ON JAVA ROAD

ON JAVA ROAD

A NOVEL

LAWRENCE OSBORNE

HOGARTH

LONDON / NEW YORK

Copyright © 2022 by Lawrence Osborne

All rights reserved.

Published in the United States by Hogarth, an imprint of Random House, a division of Penguin Random House LLC, New York.

HOGARTH is a trademark of the Random House Group Limited, and the H colophon is a trademark of Penguin Random House LLC.

LIBRARY OF CONGRESS CATALOGING-IN-PUBLICATION DATA
NAMES: Osborne, Lawrence, 1958– author.
TITLE: On Java Road / Lawrence Osborne.
DESCRIPTION: London; New York: Hogarth, [2022]
IDENTIFIERS: LCCN 2021057400 (print) | LCCN 2021057401 (ebook)
| ISBN 9780593242322 (hardcover; acid-free paper) |
ISBN 9780593242339 (ebook)
SUBJECTS: LCGFT: Novels.
CLASSIFICATION: LCC PR6065.S23 O53 2022 (print) | LCC PR6065.
S23 (ebook) | DDC 823/.914—dc23/eng/20211129
LC record available at https://lccn.loc.gov/2021057400
LC ebook record available at https://lccn.loc.gov/2021057401

Printed in Canada on acid-free paper

randomhousebooks.com

9 8 7 6 5 4 3 2 1

FIRST EDITION

Book design by Barbara M. Bachman

For NATALIE WANG

Who walked with me over the mountain to Shek O

And gave rise to a story

A GENTLEMAN ALWAYS ACTS
ACCORDING TO HIS CONSCIENCE.

—MAO TSE-TUNG,
AS REPORTED BY HIS
PHYSICIAN DR. LI ZHISUI

ON JAVA ROAD

ONE

I THOUGHT, IN THOSE DESPERATE AND FORGOTTEN days, of that passage in a novel I had read in school where the narrator insists that he prefers to be known as a reporter rather than as a journalist, the humbler word better denoting what he does, namely transcribing what he sees. Today it's an even less dishonorable job description. I knew all the journalists in Hong Kong, of course, but I also knew a fair number of the reporters—the citizens trailing the city's movable war zones, often like me all alone with a phone camera, and over time I had become more comfortable among them without consciously knowing why. But then what were we describing and for whom? I wasn't sure about that either. For myself, perhaps, and a few others scattered across the globe, such as I liked to imagine them, it would depend how deep you wanted to go into yourself. Some of these reporters had become strangely famous.

They were unlike me in that respect. Although I had been in Hong Kong for more than twenty years, slaving away as a reporter factotum gradually persevering his way into higher echelons of respectability, I had never made a name for myself in my adopted city. People knew me vaguely as a writer of something or other, and a fairly infamous glutton, but little more than that. I had gone there when still a young man, chilled to the marrow by London and its prospects and, more important, unable to see myself succeeding in that tomb of a city. I had arrived in Hong Kong just after the Handover, knowing nobody except my old university friend Jimmy Tang, and equipped only with a single suitcase and savings of five thousand sterling. I had done well given those inauspicious beginnings, but I had never become a star writer. And in a way I didn't mind at all. I had worked for a variety of newspapers, enjoyed a stint as a restaurant critic, married and divorced, accumulated a small apartment, and perfected the Chinese I had studied at university. In other words, I was an excellent nonentity.

IN FACT, AT THE beginning of that summer, when the disturbances had first erupted, I felt as though I were being woken from a deep and meaningless sleep. The city I had grown so used to—comfortable, cynical, overflowing with wine dinners and white-truffle events—was shattered the first moment I saw one of my neighbors wander onto Java Road at midnight in a white sleeveless shirt wielding a butcher's knife. I knew the man by face if not by name because I saw him every other day at Fung Shing, the restaurant on that same Java Road where I spent much of my time drinking tea with *guan tang jiao* soupy dumplings and editing my reports. I think he recognized me, too, but I was invisible to him in that moment on the street at midnight because he was there looking for protestors to intimidate, and a Chinese civil war doesn't automatically include European drifters.

Later, it was true, certain expatriated foreigners would indeed become local heroes in the conflict that consumed the city that summer, like the Frenchman with no legs who declared his solidarity with the students while standing precariously on his prostheses and orating to thrilling effect. I never found out his name, though I was resolved to buy him a drink if I ever saw him eating alone in a cheap restaurant. He was known merely as the Frenchman with No Legs. As for the fellow knife-wielding diner at Fung Shing, I never knew his name either, but he would reappear like the ghost in a folktale, never losing his power to disquiet.

He was one of the countless Fujianese immigrants concentrated in North Point, the neighborhood where I lived, which had long been a bastion of pro-Beijing nationalist sentiment. Still speaking Mandarin instead of Cantonese, they were an island among the sea of Hong Kongers who otherwise barely noticed them. Their moment of vindicating the Motherland had come, and when they achieved critical mass—as for example at Fung Shing at about 9 p.m.—they acquired a belligerent confidence even as they were huddled around pots of tea and after-dinner doughnuts, a delicacy carried from table to table on sugary trays after the main courses had been served. Since they regarded foreigners with suspicion at the best of times, and now associated us with the demonic prospect of democracy, I wondered if they, and he, were now my enemy. And even if they had drawn no blood from me personally, how should I report and describe them? This question made me want to eat at Fung Shing every single night. Besides, the very name in English, Phoenix City, now seemed more apposite than it had before. Another phoenix, another riddle.

Every time I climbed up the staircase to the second-floor eatery, which was level with its red-and-blue street sign, past a regal gold image of the bird equipped with a blue electric eye, I wondered if all eyes would be upon me as I entered the main room alone, dazzled by the overhead interrogation lights the Chinese seem to love in their restaurants, and which made me even more aware than usual of my unforgivable foreignness. I decided to call the Unknown Meat Cleaver Man Mr. Li, since that is one of the most common surnames on the mainland. If I were to ever meet him again in a dark street in those parts I wanted my assassin to have a name. *Cloven in twain by Mr. Li.* I rarely saw him at Fung Shing after that hot night of bastinadoes and disorder, men running after boys and girls in black with bamboo canes, then being chased back the same way when the momentum swung, like a theatrical production that had lost control of itself.

But it wasn't only that. As a foreigner my relation to the people eating at Fung Shing had changed almost overnight. The entire atmosphere of the city had shifted. The cadences of the language around me sharpened, a language that I had never mastered in any case. Yet I detected these changes like magnetic alterations in the airwaves.

I knew how to say "fuck your mother," *diao ni lao mu,* but now I heard it made into a sentence directed at the armored cops: *diao ni lao mu gao gun,* where the last two words could be rendered as "dog officer." The phrase *hak ging* was everywhere—dirty cops, black cops. The cops were soon shouting obscenities back at their satirists. Some of them said it in Mandarin. *Cao ni mao.* Over the warmer months the tensions that had begun with protests against an extradition law imposed by Beijing had escalated and spiraled out of control. Now, as it became more irrational, more primal, one could see a hatred operating through words as much as through beatings and tear gas. Words are the most efficient vessel for carrying the seeds of violence. The tongue contains no bones, as the Arabs say, yet it breaks bones. Everything in the depths of the mind flows effortlessly through bone-shattering words. When a cop says to a sixteen-year-old girl *sei bat po*— "die, bitch"—the violence is already performed. A verb is not an act, but it is the prelude to one, a permission the violator has granted to himself by uttering the obscenity. Once during a standoff the police used a formal warning and the girls on the front line cried back, "Come here and we'll scratch your balls off." To which there was no answer. In that moment at least, the verbal insult nullified even a barrage of rubber bullets.

For the next few days I didn't go to the daily street protests. I went to Phoenix City as usual because I relished the arctic air-conditioning and the feeling of normalcy it bestowed on its patrons. It was a relief. I sat there by one of the mirrored columns and ate salted duck yolks and soupy dumplings until the street had cooled a little, and I could go down again of sane mind and walk around the sloped streets that run up from Java Road in search of rioters, protestors—call them what you will. But none appeared. A lull had descended, as if the students, with their last wills and testaments sewn inside their jackets, had decided to take a few days off to recuperate, allowing the streets to return to being places of consumerist ease. Or, in the case of Java Road, a place of funeral homes filled with black bunting and monochrome banners haunted by the ghosts of the sugar magnates who had once made their fortunes on the maritime trade with Java, and whose imposing offices once stood here as a symbol of colonial magnanimity.

The heat rose and by midday the inhabitants of the city bore it with raised newspapers and parasols. They were glum and stoic in their minimal clothes, and I wandered down to the ferry terminal behind the Vic Hotel just to soak up the coolness of the ocean. From there, the interval of ordinariness was impressive in its potency. The junks with their mulberry sails, the lights of the Kerry Hotel across the water coming on at dusk, the ferries packed with miserable perspirers bearing fans, and the edges of the mountains a color of old tea at the end of daylight. It was around this time that bodies had begun to appear in those same waters, quietly retrieved by police boats that reporters were not permitted to approach, the first intimations of a new form of intimidation, a new configuration of the chessboard.

I sometimes retreated into the Vic, which was popular with middle-class mainlanders and since renamed, and went up to the somnambulant bar on the roof to watch the sunsets. I even brought my trunks on occasion and took an illegal dip in the hotel pool among the slightly nervous couples from the other side of the border. I suppose it was a matter of anywhere *but* my stifling little apartment at the Garland. Yet I was never lonelier than when I was in my own neighborhood and nowhere was more lonely than the top of the Vic Hotel as night came down.

IT WAS THERE THAT I used to think of Jimmy Tang and the days many years before when we had studied together at Clare College, Cambridge, and, among other things, had worked together in our spare time on a translation of Li Po's "The Exile's Letter." It was one of the most famous Chinese poems of the Tang period, perhaps the most famous, erratically translated by Ezra Pound, and our desire to embark on a new version was inspired by the fact that Pound himself had not been able to speak a word of Chinese. We found this amusing, if not preposterous. He had merely used the notes of the American scholar Ernest Fenollosa. And yet, Jimmy used to say, his interpretations were almost as haunting as the original. Beyond that, his translations of Li Po had introduced Chinese poetry to Western readers for the first time. How could it be? Pound had, however, invented the title for English-readers, as well as turning the poet's correct name— Li Bai—into "Li Po." The original was "Remembering Our Excursion in the Past: A Letter Sent to Commissary Yen of Ch'ao County."

Jimmy was a scion of one of Hong Kong's wealthiest families, and I was a scholarship boy from a small town no one has ever heard of. But being at university together had made us equals. Now, more or less a quarter of a century later, we were friends again in the very different environment of Hong Kong, and the gap, of course, had reappeared. He was a millionaire socialite, I was a struggling—and one could fairly say declining—reporter. Even when we were undergraduates I had sensed that he was someone who might slip between your fingers and disappear, even though he had always appeared so radiantly solid, so armed with life's gifts. Even then, among only a handful of people studying Chinese in that medieval university, we had shared some kind of mental territory that was invisible to other people. Tenuously, we still did.

I recall a morning in October when we had just started our first term: I caught sight of him crossing the college court. Only eighteen, a little younger than myself, he was walking in cricket whites with a Chinese girl toward the river, his shoulders draped in a cable sweater, leaving behind him a strange trail of water drops on the paving. They looked as if they were drenched from head to foot, as if they had been for a swim in the very river they were now walking toward. Alone in a little cell, I was the friendless provincial state-school boy studying Chinese because it was exquisitely unfashionable but, to me at least, also a seductively unattainable subject. And it wouldn't be an exaggeration to say that this couple trailing drops and holding hands in the shadows of the Clare court were unlike anyone else that I had ever encountered.

Later that term, after we had become acquaintances, Jimmy gave me a copy of Izaak Walton's *The Compleat Angler,* which his father in Hong Kong had in turn given to him when he was fourteen. Therein was the observation, well known to anglers over the centuries, about the sadistic use of frogs as bait: "Use him as though you loved him, that is, harm him as little as you may possibly, that he may live the longer."

You could see why a ruthless billionaire father would give such a book to his son, and why Jimmy would carry it around with him as he went to study among England's lazy elite. At the time, however, he simply said that it was the wisest book he could imagine for learning how to live, since life really was like fishing. It required patience, cunning, and an ability to sit still for long periods, paying attention to unmoving waters. It encouraged a taste for quiet killing. *The Compleat Angler*'s other advantage was that no one else in Hong Kong had ever read it. It was secret knowledge, a manual of guile and persuasion. Latterly, I never mentioned that book to him because it felt like a slightly precious affectation on the part of Tang father and son. I wondered if he still thumbed through it at critical moments.

When you look back on who you were when you were eighteen, just before the corruption sets in, you're bound to make a small and unconvincing monument out of it that shines only during restless nights when you cannot sleep. You need to slightly falsify your vanished self, to varnish him. But at the same time it's that eighteen-year-old self, cast off like an old skin, by whom you should be judged whenever you look in the mirror. He is the only judge who matters. Do you continue to disappoint him? Can there be any other outcome? What would he say to you?

When I looked back it was obvious why we had become friends at Clare. Neither of us belonged in that environment. The trappings of the English upper classes were not ours. Jimmy already had his position in the wider world because, although he came from a colony, it was a rich and vital one. It was I who was the peasant. A peasant who had learned to turn verbs in Chinese, but a peasant nonetheless.

I like to think he felt sorry for me; maybe he did. Or else I was the frog with a hook in its mouth and he was the one harming me as little as possible. I would see him every day at lectures and in Mandarin classes and, as is the way with students, it only took a couple of weeks before we were on nodding and then speaking terms. By Christmas of first year we were going to the Eagle every evening, or Waffles on Fitzroy Street, or the Indian next to New Hall, and he had assumed over me the senior position—better clothes, better hair, more spending power, and more literary candlepower. It was the head start that the rich always enjoy. Fast out of the blocks, they can be outpaced only later in life, when it's usually too late. I calculate that it gives them a fifteen-year advantage, which is the span of time needed to at least draw level with them. By contrast, they often burn out early. If you surpass them later in life they will always complain that their early advantage was, in reality, a handicap. Jimmy, however, would never suffer that disillusion. Although his father already had his future mapped out to the last detail, Jimmy told me that he'd declared to the patriarch even before he had left for Cambridge that he had decided to become a scholar of Tang poetry—and there was nothing his vile clan could do to stop him. "They're all psychopaths and spendthrifts anyway," he said to me, as if I were the only person to whom he would ever say such things, though he later repeated them obsessively in Hong Kong. "I have an uncle who has a different car for every day of the week. Color coded. My grandfather made his money in the gambling dens in the '40s. They were racketeers from Shanghai, that's all. It's what I am, too, if you look hard enough."

He was fond of reminding me that the first British cemeteries in Hong Kong specifically excluded the Chinese dead. "But you let us in eventually—as corpses." His English, acquired at the Diocesan Boys' School on Argyle Street in Hong Kong, was faultless and almost without accent. He never talked about his years at Millfield school later on, and I learned never to ask him about them. He was more interested in my school, a secondary modern in the English countryside. *That* was true exoticism for him. He was fascinated by the class machinery behind such an establishment. When I told him that I had passed much of my teenage years being groomed to be a qualified mechanic, he nodded and said, "Yes, that might have been better. Now you'll have nothing but a useless Chinese Studies degree. And who among Western literates even reads Chinese poetry these days?" It was possible that he didn't believe this other hypothetical future. But one look at my disgusting clothes—the eyebrow rose— and he understood that there might be some truth to it. Clothes. It was why we first began going to London. Clothes were never trivial to him, as they never are to truly serious people. When talking about Maoism, for example, he would just grimace and say, "Yes, yes, I understand, but the clothes, comrade, the *clothes*."

He got me fitted at Dege and Skinner and bought me hats at Lock and Co. that were, I thought at the time, too old for me but which he gave me the confidence to wear. I was the only person in my year to own a panama hat who had the gall to actually wear it. I found that I didn't know my own capital city at all, but Jimmy knew it intimately from a thousand Tang family expeditions. I didn't know anything about anything. I had never been to a restaurant there. Never spent a night in a hotel, never drunk wine, never taken a black cab, never been to a nightclub or a theater, and had never been to any site of note except for the British Museum and Karl Marx's grave in Highgate Cemetery, taken to them by my grandfather: the high-minded pilgrimages of the working class. It would have been difficult to describe to Jimmy the scene with the old man, a retired bus driver from Bevendean, standing before the Zardoz-like head of Marx in the rain. He, eyes filled with tears, his arms piled with votive flowers; me, shivering and unmoved behind him. Jimmy Tang, scion of a family who had fled the Communists in China, would have quipped that at least Jewish Marxists got to be buried there.

For Jimmy, my "reeducation" was a *Pygmalion* game, which he played with an inborn skill. It kept me in my place, though in a subtle and often unnoticeable way. And yet it also let him—perversely—into the English social game to which even Millfield had never opened the doors. But then again, there was Chinese poetry, that cathedral in the landscape of words. It was with Jimmy that I learned to recite it correctly and to sink into its rhythms. The poem about seeing off Meng Haoran at Yellow Crane Tower was the first Li Bai he taught me to recite, making me similar to a billion Chinese school-children, though he never followed through on his vow to write a translation that would surpass Pound's famous English version. For how would you improve *The smoke flowers are blurred over the river?*

TWO

THE TANGS LIVED BELOW MAGAZINE GAP ROAD IN THE Mid-Levels in a building called Borrett Mansions. These fortress-like luxury tower blocks stood at the end of a narrow lane called Bowen Road, which burrowed through tropical forest crowded with creeper vines and ficus roots as it rose toward the rusticated walls of the Mansions. Here, on the ground floor of which were surprisingly modest Art Deco–style lobbies, it felt as if time had stood still since about 1970. Raised high above the city, the air around the Mansions smelled of moss and wet bark, and a mountain chill touched my face as soon as I got out of the car. It had rained just an hour before. The hillside of ferns and creepers around me dripped quietly as I walked across the back entrance lane to the lobby that served their apartment on the fifteenth floor.

A doorman was already there ahead of me with the door held open. He knew me and skipped to the elevator, knowing already which ivory button to press. But I had never learned his name. As I stood by the metal frame of the elevator, in tune with its 1930s British style, he looked me up and down as if deciding whether my shoes were good enough. A weekend night on the Mid-Levels and in politically uncertain times. I would have guessed most of the wealthy inhabitants of the Mansions were already elsewhere in the world. The money was flowing outward, an unstoppable tide driven by despair at what was unfolding in their city. When the doors opened, however, a maid was there to greet arrivals. Recalling me, she said, "How are you, Mr. Gyle?" as we traveled up to the people richer than we were, exchanging a look of shared melancholy.

It was a gathering of about fifteen people, a dinner more than a party. But the Tangs didn't like sitting around a table and so guests were served anywhere they happened to be seated. I, too, liked it that way. They were knowing hosts and made no missteps when it came to entertaining at home. Melissa Tang opened the door; clearly, the doorman had announced me. She was in a black cashmere cardigan and velvet trousers, casual for her, and because they were the same color the only thing the eye noticed was her collar of pearls. It was dramatic and chic; she was always like that. It was also the old apartment of her father, the eccentric millionaire Rodney Chow, and its carpeted rooms and Ming terra-cottas collected from China made her comfortable. The Chows were as wealthy as the Tangs, though they had made their money in manufacturing and television stations. Rodney, a cantankerous old-timer fond of jacquard smoking jackets and Swedish girls, was often to be seen both at the Tangs' soirees and about town, though I rarely interacted with him since I feared and disliked him. Rodney's outsize taste was everywhere apparent. One of those priceless terra-cottas was a life-size horse, its neck garlanded with earthy bells, standing like a guardian deity in the vestibule. Whenever Melissa walked past it she ran a hand softly along its flank, as she did now. "I'm so glad you came," she said, not turning to me as she led me in. "Jimmy's been in a foul mood all day."

"Oh?"

"The family want him to make a statement about the Hong Kong situation so that the authorities know where we stand—with them, hopefully."

"A statement?"

"They want him to declare his loyalty to the state and to the Communist Party. Well, it wouldn't be worded like that."

"How would it be worded, then?"

She vacillated inwardly, I could see it, and her mouth set as her teeth ground together and she mustered all her diplomacy.

"It would be worded as a declaration of belief—in the future of Hong Kong. Do I have to spell it out?"

Over the years I had come to think of their home as the most elegant in Hong Kong, even though it was old-fashioned, creaky in its way, and stripped of modern technology. It was deliberately Victorian because that had been Melissa's father's more Western taste, but gradually her own, more Chinese sensibility had begun to prevail. The chandeliers were statically ominous, the wall tapestries showed Forbidden City scenes that I couldn't place stylistically, suspended between Orientalism and the actual East, and the terra-cottas were now everywhere, raised on pedestals or shelved inside niches, museum quality and a shade too proud of themselves. They lay among a handful of delicate Luis Chan psychedelic watercolors from the late 1960s depicting dreamy islands and ghosts alongside trippy dinosaurs and strange-looking birds, and a single more controversial Chow Chun Fai piece in contemporary neorealist style that Jimmy had forced his wife to accept. I knew that Chun Fai painted stills from classic Hong Kong movies of decades past and that his anti-establishment politics made him unwelcome to people of Melissa's background—yet the piece hung in their sitting room almost unnoticed, in a spirit of uneasy compromise. A group of men seated around a table in undershirts playing cards in some forgotten year of the 1970s, exuding a quiet threat.

This room opened onto a balcony, which basked in the glow of the never-sleeping towers that descended toward Victoria Harbour. The sea appeared and the neons of Tsim Sha Tsui burned on its black surface as ferries passed through the reflections. There was a group already seated there in the wicker chairs drinking Manhattan Iced Tea out of communal jugs. I knew quite a few of them. The Tangs had two circles that overlapped awkwardly: high-rolling hedge funders and bankers on the one hand, and journalists and academics who journeyed up to the exotic world of the Mid-Levels to mingle with these financial overlords, who in turn barely noticed them. I was familiar with both circles, though I preferred the bankers, in a way. They were less pretentious and their kindly fascism was cheerily upfront.

But meanwhile there was a second balcony, which Jimmy had turned into a tropical garden, entered by a different room, and Melissa took me there now because she wanted to have a word with me alone, if I didn't mind. The view was the same, yet we sat alone together on the single sofa that stood within that miniature jungle. One of the maids brought us drinks. I was not especially close to Melissa, though obviously we had known each other for years through Jimmy. I found her sympathetic and, in her way, brittlely noble. It wasn't her stoic endurance of Jimmy's childishness and selfishness that was noble, but rather her capacity to pretend that she thought certain things for the sake of a higher cause. She would extol the efficiency of the Chinese Communist Party when it came to building highways or managing to put a rover on the dark side of the moon. She didn't really believe as the Party did, that such efficiency mattered, but she did believe in the nation's ascent and its long, continually evolving glory, which would guarantee, one day, a hegemonic future. More important, it would be her future, too, and her family's. Most people would call that hypocrisy or worse, since it was clear that she was not entirely convinced that communism itself was the all-encompassing beatitude of the future. But there are more worldly ways of understanding it. Her duty was to her clan, her dynasty, her people, and her civilization—as she saw it. It was not a political loyalty. It was deeper than that and therefore more tenacious. It was a loyalty weary but unswerving, and it made me admire her in spite of myself. She always thought me aimless, a rootless wanderer, and deep down I knew that she was right.

"It's been awhile since I've seen you," Melissa said in her half-formal way, crossing her legs and trying her best to look relaxed. It wasn't easy for her. "I'm sorry I wasn't here the last time you came up. Jimmy says you've been working for a high and mighty news organization."

"Well, it isn't CNN."

"I'm glad to hear it. We have quite enough American propaganda here as it is. I'm pleased for you either way. When I get some time I'll read your dispatches."

I was rather hoping she wouldn't, because the last thing I wanted with her were political discussions when we both knew how we felt about the issues. I was typically evangelical for democracy while she, a patriotic older type, couldn't think of anything worse. So I prevaricated with a little self-denigration but her eyes were bright and had seen right into me.

"I am a bit worried about Jimmy," she went on smoothly, with a metronome's ease. "He's been behaving a little on the odd side lately. Have you noticed?"

"The odd side?"

"Mood swings. I was hoping—well, not hoping exactly, but I was thinking you might have an insight into it. I know you two play tennis every week. Don't you have dinner at the China Club, too?"

"Sometimes."

"You must have picked up on something? We're all a bit tense lately, but my father was asking about him the other day."

"I take it he's worried Jimmy has *wrong opinions*?"

She shrugged. "Oh, he can have whatever opinions he likes, for heaven's sake. It's not that. But he can't break ranks."

"Break ranks with your family?"

"You know what I mean. We have some standing with the Party, as I'm sure you understand." She stared at me, lowered her voice. "We can't have Jimmy going all pro-democracy on us."

"I'm sure it's not that."

"A woman, then?"

It was time to force a laugh. No woman, I insisted.

But her tone remained flat, probing:

"It must be something else, then."

Pausing, she looked away from me into the glow of crayon-kit neons and the motion of ships whose decks were lit up like floating weddings. There was something in this vista that rejuvenated her train of thought. I decided to keep talking:

"We don't talk about much on the personal level. Men don't tend to, contrary to all the mythology."

"I don't believe that for a moment."

"It's true in our case. Either way, he hasn't mentioned anything. He's not drinking that heavily as far as I can tell."

"He's a tiresome philanderer, I know that. You don't have to pretend otherwise to me. And I don't want you to squeal on him. But I'd appreciate it if you kept an eye on him for me. For *us*. The whole family is concerned. He and my father had a vicious row the other night."

"About what?"

"Jimmy's behavior, his recklessness. People see him around town associating with all sorts of *people*—it's not a good moment for public scandals."

"There's hardly a scandal hanging over you. One shouldn't get too excited."

"Not yet. But you can feel these things coming. I wanted to ask if you had any inkling of where it might come from."

"Me?" I had to fend this off with a theatrical laugh.

"It's not a crazy question," she insisted. "From my point of view—"

"There's nothing I've seen, Melissa. He's not going to secret political meetings. He's not taking movie actresses to a hidden-away love nest."

He was probably doing both but I held her eye and gradually she seemed to calm down.

"All right. But I'd be grateful if you could come to me if you feel there's something I should know. Would you do that for me?"

I had to say yes, and I had to at least partially mean it. Over the years her family had been welcoming to me. They had invited me to their parties, their dinners, they had put in a good word for me here and there behind closed doors. I would go further: they had been one of my lifelines into the Hong Kong establishment. Not that I was an insider in that world, far from it. But I could drop into it from time to time, as an interloper, and this ability was in large measure due to them. Since the Tangs were shipping billionaires, and donated charitably on a remarkable scale, they were not only amiable friends to me, but extremely useful ones as well. Jimmy's father was kinder to me than Rodney Chow and well aware of how long I had known his son and how much affection existed between us.

"You've reassured me," she said, smoothing down her already unruffled trousers, as if the velvet had accumulated motes of dust I couldn't see. "Shall we have some punch?"

For the rest of the evening I didn't see much of Jimmy until the party had thinned and the remnants gathered again on the balcony. Then he appeared suddenly in one of his beautiful W. W. Chan suits, an ecru herringbone number made from a Dugdale Lisburn linen. Elegance came spontaneously to him. He shot me a knowing look, seeing that I had spotted what he wanted me to notice about his appearance.

The others were mostly men who had known his father and who liked to talk quietly and cynically among themselves with Jimmy's magnums of Domaine de Montille Volnay, decanted for an hour before being served. They were mostly pro-China in their views, *servants of stability,* as Jimmy called them. Many of them had companies in Shanghai and Shenzhen. Like Swire or the Ho family, they knew which side of their toast was buttered by their masters in Beijing. At the same time they also knew how to make themselves sound patriotically reasonable and capitalistically moderate. Once they had reviled communism; now they dismissed it as irrelevant. Yet in a bizarre twist of historical fate they were now quoting Western leftists with veiled approval because, among those same leftists, conspiracy theories about CIA intervention in China and hatred of imperialism were naturally second nature. These theories chimed conveniently with the oligarchs' own financial self-interest. It was a performance that I had heard many times before: out there, down in the city, the younger generation was spoiling their paradise, and they resented being called "collaborators" and "traitors" by their own grandchildren when in their eyes it was they who had built the city and not their ungrateful spawn.

But as they got drunker their tempers flared less and they fell to reminiscing. Their families were all connected by blood and business and they shared a great deal of lore.

Funny uncles and mad great-aunts, once-graceful cousins who had gone to the dogs and family misers whom no one had seen for years. Dynastic money flowed through them like the sap of a giant ancient tree. This all went on for a while as I sat there in a corner listening to them and sipping my portion of Jimmy's cellar, wondering when they would all go home and leave Jimmy and me alone in our regal state.

When it did eventually happen, they departed rather abruptly. Left behind was a French friend of Jimmy's whom I had met before and who always came to his parties dressed *à la chinoise* and who sold Melissa artworks, as far as could be known. Olivier Metz looked like a Qing courtier in his silk jackets and white socks—did he ever dress like that for the mall?—and he held court for a while, telling us all that people calling for independence and the disbanding of the police force should remember that Hong Kong had to buy nearly all its water from mainland China, and that the activists had no doubt failed to come up with a serious water plan. They were naive fools and utopians.

"It's easy to wreck a few train stations. But what do they do when the taps run dry?"

"It's just vandalism for its own sake," Melissa added imperiously.

"In my opinion," Olivier went on, "it's a generation that has been brought up on Western propaganda. No one can do anything about it because it's the media the young live on. They don't even understand what they're dismantling."

"But wait a minute," Jimmy said, about to enjoy a dig at his wife, "we pay through the nose for that water. And we are forced by China to throw the excess into the sea because we are not allowed to store it. That's a racket right there. We're supposed to be grateful for that?"

"Where would you prefer to get your water, then?" the Frenchman said.

"I'd rather buy it from Taiwan, since you ask. They have plenty. What do you think, Adrian?" All eyes turned to me. "Our friend here covers the protests every day. He knows far more about it than we do."

"Not at all," I said. "I'm the foreigner here."

Jimmy said, not quite seriously, "You Brits were the ones who founded Hong Kong. It's perverse, but you not only have the right to an opinion, it would be cowardly if you *didn't* offer one. Everything that's going on today is about you as well. You are in this disgusting mix. It's an Anglo-Chinese fuckup."

"I'm not a nativist," Melissa said, smiling at me. "We're all immigrants here, after all."

I knew all about how Rodney Chow's family had emigrated from Shanghai in '49, like so many others, and for that matter Jimmy's grandparents as well. The loan sharks, gunrunners, or black marketeers that they must have originally been, hard men running contraband boats under the cover of darkness before they graduated to more respectable ventures.

I began, and gave a bland account of my days on the front line. There wasn't a long story to tell but I knew there was something exotic about it to them. Their distance from it made it satisfyingly pornographic. Yet this class was itself in two minds; many of them outwardly critical of the upheavals but quietly supporting them in private. They were caught in a paradox. Practically speaking, what exactly do you do when it turns out that your attractive way of life shifts on its foundations and suddenly appears to rest upon something completely unfamiliar? Foundations that you did not grow up with beneath your feet, to say the least. You don't give up that way of life. You justify the new reality to yourself. Now, comically, the Communist Party was the secret to their capitalist serenity. Metz was good at this reframing. President Xi was a classic emperor, as Mao had been, and if one day he had eunuchs and harems and courtiers—as Mao had insisted upon—it wouldn't be surprising. The imperium was the imperium and its stability was more valuable than freedom of speech and a benevolent police force with no guns. Bondage to the state was not the worst thing one could imagine so long as it kept you safe and fed, which it usually did.

"So do slaves," Jimmy drawled, "get to love their little cages."

"But Monsieur Jimmy, do I look like a slave?"

"I can't speak for you, Olivier."

I was longing for him to leave so that Jimmy and I could talk alone. It was midnight before we were in the clear. Melissa went to bed with her earplugs inserted, which left the two of us and the two maids clearing up the debris of a slightly unsatisfying evening.

It was cigar time. Jimmy opened a walnut box on the coffee table and took out two Cohibas for us.

"It's always the best moment of the evening, when all the bores and the boors have left. My amateur salon used to be so entertaining. What happened?"

"The regulars stopped coming."

"It's cruel to say but I suppose it's hard to deny the truth. Everyone's abroad. Soon it'll just be us." He puffed on his cigar. "It wouldn't be so bad. I wouldn't mind it at all, as a matter of fact. Shall we finish the Montille—I kept some of it aside from the Visigoths."

He asked one of the maids to bring two new glasses and we finished the cigars before dipping in. It was wine heresy, the smoke ruining the mouth, but he wanted to finish the bottle that night. During the course of the evening something had gotten to him. Sometimes, in the course of our long friendship, I was the person he would come to when he wanted to get something off his chest, and this was occasionally true of matters concerning his tortuous love life. Such was the case now.

"There's a wonderful woman I want you to meet." His tone shifted and I could tell that he was tiptoeing toward a delicate subject. "Her name is Rebecca To. She's a student, and yes, I know you'll judge me about that, but sometimes that's the way things turn out. Don't be judgmental. Anyway, I invited her out on the yacht and she came along. Seems she's some sort of literature student, though of course now they're all on strike. At first I thought we'd have nothing in common—she's much more political than me and a bit fierce with the student movement. But I got past that. When I met her I was struck by the famous lightning strike of the heart, the pure electricity smacking you in the chest. You know how that is. You feel like you're about to have a stroke. Anyway, I'd like you to meet her. There's something about her."

So, I thought, Melissa's hunch had been unerringly correct.

I said, "How old is she? Twenty-one or something?"

"Twenty-three, actually. She's a year or two behind." He glanced down at his nails for a moment. "I didn't say anything dramatic happened. I just had her out to dinner. I'm supposed to meet her on Thursday night—I think you should come with us. Melissa will be at a charity ball in Macao."

"This Thursday night?"

"Don't be stiff about it, Adriano." That's what he always called me when he wanted something. "Don't tell me you're going to be at home writing your memoirs. You're just going to waste your time propping up a bar and sitting in front of your TV. Come with us to Duddell's."

"You want a second opinion, is that it?"

Sheepishly, he avoided my eye for a moment.

"Maybe I'm infatuated. It happens at our age. Pathetic, I know. But not entirely pathetic."

"Delusional, perhaps?"

"Yes, a bit of that. I don't mind being delusional rather than pathetic. There are worse things to be. It all depends what you are delusional about, don't you think?"

"Delusions serving some noble end, you mean? Like chasing after students?"

He smiled grimly. "You've got me there. But all the same—so what? So what if we delude ourselves with girls who are too young to love us back? They're just as cruel as we are. Everyone is selfish, and if you think about it we can't be otherwise. Why make a fuss about it? We're all going to die a few years from now—at least you and I will. I'm philosophical about it, as they say. Besides, I'm not going to lose my head over her."

"Isn't being infatuated losing your head?" I was irritating him and enjoying the effect.

"Yes, but there are different ways of losing one's head. Anyway, we don't have any control over these things. Coups de foudre and all that. If I'm smitten, I'm smitten. I have been smote. I just want you to throw some cold water in my face if it's needed. I didn't get the impression that she's the gold-digger sort."

Then I asked him offhandedly about her name. Wasn't Rebecca rather unusual as a first name? But then I remembered another Rebecca in Hong Kong society, a friend of the Cantopop singer and actor Leslie Cheung whose last name I couldn't recall. I remembered Cheung, that great gay icon of my youth, the androgynous star of *Days of Being Wild* and *A Better Tomorrow,* because after he committed suicide by jumping off the twenty-fourth floor of the Mandarin Oriental in 2003 his wake had taken place at the eastern end of Java Road, where, as I say, all the funeral parlors lay. A curious chain of associations.

"All right," I said, "I'll be there. Thursday night. But my brutal honesty will cost you dinner and whatever bottle I want."

"Deal! You know, Adrian, life is unbearable not because it's a tragedy but because it's a romance—who said that?"

I said I couldn't remember.

"And this is a romance. Though I have to admit that so far it's anything but unbearable."

There was one other thing, however.

"She's going out every night to the protests. We meet afterward, and she smells of tear gas. I admit I rather like it. It's as close as *I'll* ever get to the front line."

I blew out my mouthful of smoke and told him that was a pretty stupid thing to say, but that I wouldn't repeat it.

"It may be stupid, Adrian, but it's certainly true."

At that very moment, I had to admit, I was wondering what it must be like to be in bed with someone drenched in chloroacetophenone, the chemical used in tear gas. That odor was ubiquitous during those days and nights; it rolled down the large avenues from the late afternoon onward, settling as a faint and sour aroma in my own apartment, where it penetrated the permanently closed windows.

"Tell me," he said, "do you think she's on a suicide mission along with all her friends? It's what I tell her. It's like a collective frenzy, an ecstasy. I've become more and more interested in it. I'd never go to a protest myself, obviously, but I'm fascinated by the anarchy. It's like the birth of a new religion."

I felt the same, though there was no need to say it. It was a phenomenon of youth, and both of us knew it because in some way we were both excluded from it by our age. We could sympathize but we couldn't go down into the streets and throw rocks. Or perhaps that's just what we told ourselves to justify our inertia.

I said, "There's a kind of madness in the air which no one understands. It's generational, isn't it?"

"Isn't it always?"

"Like the late '60s. Overnight, everything disintegrates. The young no longer believe in the middle-aged."

There was something else, he went on. He had lied about meeting her haphazardly. She was from old money and their families knew each other. "There," he groaned, "it's all out in the open." I laughed and told him how ridiculous he was. As if that could have been hidden.

The maids had by now melted away and we were alone at the edge of a vast urban landscape filled with electrical ghosts, the light show of a Hong Kong night. From down in the city came the persistent cries from the high-rises of people shouting choruses of defiance as they had for an hour, a sound that had become more animal despite the words that we could clearly hear. It echoed from building to building in a chain that might have encompassed the whole city in a few minutes.

Jimmy was seemingly unmoved. He was merely curious as to why they were doing it. This must be a form of auditory semaphore bearing coded messages aimed at them, the rich and lofty in their hillside castles. Even though I told him that this was not the case, he refused to believe me and continued straining to catch the words that echoed across the ether. One of those words, undoubtedly, was *liberate,* as in *liberate Hong Kong*. *Gwong fuk heung gong*. It was a phrase invented by the activist Edward Leung. He had also coined the phrase "innovation for our generation," and later "revolution of our time." *Si doi gak ming*. But in fact it was the first time that summer I had heard "revolution of our time." For Jimmy, needless to say, it was proof that they were delusional and had no sense of material realities, since a revolution was never going to happen in a thousand years. He offered me the end of the magnum and said as much as we finished it, though

I had to guess whether his new lover was included in the generalization. He was a man who, deep down, believed that words came cheaply to most people and so constituted a debased coinage. To him, "revolution," *gak ming*, was the cheapest of the cheap especially in English, a word worthy of John Lennon and Patty Hearst. But just because it was being shouted from a high-rise at midnight by teenagers didn't mean that it was entirely debased—or that it was even used at all by people like Rebecca.

"By the way," I asked, "what is her Chinese name?"

"Luan Feng. You know what it means?"

"Phoenix."

It was a traditional name with a strong whiff of nobility. Li Bai himself used it, since for him the phoenix itself was a time-honored symbol of integrity just as it had been for Zhuangzi and the early Taoists. He admired the bird's freedom and unrestricted movement. A few images came back to me, the phoenix of Li Bai dwelling near the edge of a waterfall at dawn. But I kept that to myself and went on:

"As for me, I am *Ah di le an*, as your people call me, and that means nothing to anyone. It doesn't even sound like A-dri-an. And you are? I never found out."

"I'm not telling you, I'm superstitious about it. But *Ah di le an* suits you quite well. I'm not sure if Phoenix really suits Rebecca." So, I thought for a moment, the association with our shared poet had not even occurred to him. It was surprising since the bird was a symbol of liberation. "Besides, having an English name is useful sometimes. It's an alter ego. You can slip into it or hide behind it."

———

A LITTLE BEFORE ONE O'CLOCK Jimmy walked me back down to the lobby where the doorman I had seen before was fast asleep in front of his monitor. We stood together in the cool of the forest waiting for his driver and finishing the damp stubs of the once-noble Cohibas. In his Dugdale suit, still only slightly rumpled from the evening's frivolities, Jimmy looked like a figure from the very decade in which the Borrett Mansions had been built. A ghost suddenly emerging into the age of electrical light, an anachronism that was not quite an anachronism. It was then that I remembered how, when we were students, he had always reminded me of the Arrow Collar Man, that slick icon of male beauty invented by the American illustrator J. C. Leyendecker for *The Saturday Evening Post* in the 1920s. Elegant and idealized models for Interwoven socks, Cluett shirts, and of course the famous Arrow Collars. "Ephemera" that glowed from a distance, not quite real in the drab light of common sense and yet far more real than photographs.

He finished his stub and instead of tossing it into the nearby ficus roots darted back to the door and crushed it into the sand ashtray standing next to it.

His driver swept upon us out of nowhere. Jimmy didn't do the farewell handshake, only the welcome kind. I rode down to Kennedy Road and then was borne mindlessly toward the deep-set gloom of Wan Chai Park, the Queen Elizabeth Stadium, and the Dorsett, which I had passed the previous day. The streets were filled with little stones like the aftermath of a volcanic eruption. For some reason we went down Yee Wo

Street: elsewhere were events that had to be avoided. Around Victoria Park morose crowds were beginning to part and go their own ways, and along a wall I saw new graffiti in Chinese that read, "In this life only marry a front-liner." It was a delicious sign that Phoenix would never stay with Jimmy Tang, not forever in any case.

ALL THIS WAS RUNNING through my mind the following night as I was seated at a bar called the Old Man in Central. All through the previous twenty-four hours I had been feeling increasingly anxious, aware that I was becoming less and less invisible in the city as my outward appearance as a foreigner—as a European—began to take on new and dangerous meanings.

As I came down onto the street after six brandies I saw a lout standing at the corner of Staunton across from Fat Choy, holding himself up against the wall of steeply pitched Aberdeen Street, a man in the telltale white shirt of pro-Beijing street-gang types and emerald satin knickerbockers. He in turn caught sight of me as I waited for my car. He was holding an empty bottle of Jack Daniel's and, as if not knowing what else to do with it, lobbed it across the street at both me and my fading sharkskin suit. It smashed against the curb and tiny particles of glass landed upon the fabric of my sleeves and trousers. There was no one on the corner, but you could tell that a crowd had just passed and people had been battered; he himself had a bloody nose. He looked as if he had drunk that bottle of Jack Daniel's all by himself. The neck didn't smash for some reason and rolled away down Aberdeen, gathering speed while the man raised a fist and called me *gaat ʒaat* a cockroach. I wasn't wearing any items of clothing normally associated with the protestors, such as a black shirt, so it must have been a drunken generalization, I thought, spat out indiscriminately.

Gaat ʒaat in Cantonese had acquired a particular context during those sweltering summer weeks but I hadn't thought it would ever be used against me, not even by the counter-protesters in white shirts who until then had seemed shy with suited foreigners. They hated us and sometimes cried "CIA" as I walked by, but only when I was in combat gear. "CIA" in Mandarin sounded almost poetic: *ʒhongyang qingbaoju*. This one was out for more blood and he came hunting me, crossing the junction toward a small roadwork near Beer Fish. Staggering a little, his eyes bloodshot, he called me a cockroach again and spat on the ground while at the far end of Staunton I saw my taxi coming to save me. He was already snarling with a certain amount of melody: *Diu lei lao mu—*

Before the car reached me, he had swung a wide punch and caught me on the right cheek, but not with enough force to knock me over. It was a weakling's punch. "Easy, easy," was all I managed to say, and swore at him in French in a desperate attempt to put him off. I believe I called him a lover of prostitutes. He came at me again, displeased with a foreign expression, and it was the opened door of the taxi that rescued me from a second attempt on his part. I dived in and slammed the door behind me, more astonished than anything else. I wasn't hurt, but I was insulted. And worse than being insulted, I had been taken unawares and by surprise.

In the back seat I noticed the driver looking me over in his

rearview mirror, mildly entertained, as a pinprick of blood
had landed on the white front of my shirt and sat there like a
mortified ladybug. I wondered if it was his blood or mine,
and so I raised a finger to my cheek and discovered that it was
indeed split and bleeding. I had to use my Tie Your Tie
pocket square to staunch it, thus staining its translucent yellow butterflies.

I swore out loud and for a while forgot where I was going.
The stunned feeling of being jumped, however incompe-
tently, obliterated all else for a good ten minutes.

"*Gaat ʒaat,* " the driver said to me, grinning knowingly in
the mirror. "Him, not you. Too short ride this time, but I'll
take you anyway."

He had saved me. Foxglove was on the ground floor of an
apartment block off Queens Road Central and had a secret
door marked by a basket filled with umbrellas. It was an all-
night place with jazz, which only a man as tedious as Cunningham could have suggested, a typical journalist's idea of
a raffish spot. Who wants jazz after a scrap with a thug? I
thought glumly. Somewhere along Queen's Road Central, in
any case, I got the driver to stop and decided to walk up to
Foxglove. By the time I had found the building on Ice House
Street with its low display windows at street level, filled with
gold and silver cane handles in the shapes of duck and cat
heads, my cheek had dried out. Above the heads were signs
from another age. *Established 1868. Handmade. Repairs.*

I looked at myself in the glass displays of the cryptic
vestibule—yet more silver cane heads—and saw in the com-
promised reflection that I now had an ugly wound and that it
didn't give my face much extra character. That foul triad

member, if indeed he was one, had ruined my week and not just my evening. I should have told him that yes, I was CIA and that I carried legal firepower. Nonetheless I calmed myself and strode to the basket of umbrellas. I knew already that one had to play a little game with them. You had to push the handles down until you got the right one; having tried four of them, then, the fifth one caused something to click behind the wall of mirrors and the whole wall sprang to life and moved sideways. I stepped into a pitch-dark bar with a bandstand and a quartet playing Brubeck numbers.

One move inside and the wall slid back into place. The place was full and at the bar Charles Cunningham was installed with his sickly Cointreau among women too young to notice him. He was in the custom-made safari jacket he always wore throughout the unbearable summers, probably some piece of garbage from Sam's Tailor, where he had gone because he had seen Anthony Bourdain get a suit made there. The pockets filled with quinine pills and the sweat clinging to his face had not dried because the rolls of fat that covered his neck were ample defense against the strongest air-conditioning.

"There you are," he said, barely raising a hand to shake mine. "I thought you were coming from the Old Man."

His hand was clammy and I dropped it as soon as I could.

"I was, Cunningham, but I got attacked. A triad member threw a punch at me outside Fat Choy."

"Oh? Was there any particular reason?"

"Who knows. Maybe he was just drunk and in a bad mood."

"Highly unusual, though. There's no crime here to speak of."

"The moron was waiting outside for me with a bottle of Jack Daniel's. Maybe he'd had an argument with his wife."

"Or tensions are high—and whites are the enemy for those types."

"Perhaps."

"Have a drink, you poor boy."

"I'll have a sling. I have a mind to go back and fuck him up."

"Don't do that. It's triads who fuck *us* up, not the other way around. Come on, just sit down and let the blood dry."

"I should have swung back at him."

"It's what one always thinks after getting punched. But you didn't because you were scared. As Mike Tyson used to say—"

"Like hell I was. He threw a bloody bottle at me."

"—everyone has a plan until they get punched in the face."

The sling arrived and, having waited for it politely, Cunningham offered a toast to injured journalists and I to Tong Boon, the bartender at Raffles in Singapore who invented the sling before the First World War.

"Those were the days," I said as grandly as I could, my hand still slightly shaking with rage at my humiliation, "and they'll never come back. *Yam sing*." I downed the whole thing and slammed the glass back on the bar. "Barman, one more *mgoi sai*."

"Are you flush, Gyle?"

"Flush? Why on earth would I be flush?"

"You look flush. You're behaving flush."

"Not flush exactly but *The Raven* paid me for my piece about racetracks finally. It's been four months. It's just an extra thousand bucks for drinking in any case. I have to be flush to hang out with you. It's like being friends with a cash-eating vertical wind tunnel."

"Well, if you say so. Barman, one more, *mgoi*."

I said that as far as I could see this place was full of "locusts"—it was our term for journalists and bloggers who had flown in from all over the world to cover the troubles in our city but who otherwise had little idea where they were and cared even less. It was also a Cantonese word for main-landers. Both species were seated in the dark with girls they had picked up somewhere. The Western species in their gar-ishly bad journalist clothes: Banana Republic shirts and or-thopedic shoes, as much the dregs of former glories as we were ourselves. The mainlanders in suits they had bought at Sam's.

"They let them in at the airport," Cunningham said, "and there's nothing we can do about it. It's competition, Gyle."

"Yes, it's a calamity all right. Where is the police state when you need it? Is this what we pay taxes for?"

"They parachute in and take all the girls." He glanced around. "It's piracy."

I raised a hand to my wound and felt the hardening scab tighten the skin over my cheekbone. The triad man had aimed well, like a professional. It was well known that triads recruited from the ranks of amateur boxers, in much the same way that the authorities recruited from among them when they needed shock troops to beat up the unwarlike rebels. So it was probably true that cowardice on this occasion had been the better part of valor. Gradually, however, the gin sedated me and the good mood I had been in three hours earlier returned. I had been with Sheila Ng from Reuters and at one point it had seemed that I might have some success with her—but she had taken the first opportunity to vanish into thin air and the Old Man had not yielded a replacement. I was getting noticeably older. Charm and rapier wit alone were no longer enough. Nevertheless the day had not been entirely wasted. I had spent most of the afternoon interviewing a lawmaker who could barely control his eagerness for an imminent crackdown. I asked Cunningham where he had been.

"I took the day off and went to Dragon's Back. I took the taxi all the way there and when I got to the top of the mountain I remembered that I can't hike because I'm too fat. You see, my lack of fitness is finally taking its toll on me—"

"You should take up Pilates."

His eyes went into tonic immobility.

"Oh, what kind? I've heard Pontius is the best version of it."

"Stern and judgmental. *That's* what you need."

Only I laughed, though. He had a comedian's delivery. *Pontius Pilates.*

He asked me what I was up to these days. Who was I seeing?

"No one really. Though I'm meeting Jimmy Tang on Thursday."

"Tang? Don't you know him from university?"

"Decades ago. It's only because of him that I'm here at all. Did you ever meet him?"

"Too 'beautiful people' for me. I just follow him in the gossip rags."

I said, "He can never get himself out of those gossip columns. The fact that he's widely hated is what makes me trust him. We'll have dinner with him one day and you can make your mind up for yourself."

"Well, you better hope your face gets better by tomorrow. It's starting to swell up."

From one moment to the next his face tensed with concern and he peered at the wound as if it had worsened second by second before his eyes.

"You should go to the hospital and have that cleaned up. What if it's infected?"

All because of a drunk triad, I thought.

I looked at my watch, as if it mattered.

"I could take a car up to Canossa and have it looked at."

"Let's have another round and you can tell them it's normal for you—you're an alcoholic."

"I was probably tipsy when he hit me."

Cunningham told me that *Time* magazine might be pulling him out at the end of the year and sending him to Jakarta. His twelve years of enjoying life in Hong Kong, playing the Great White Correspondent, were perhaps coming to an end and he would descend back into Purgatory either in Jakarta or eventually a suburb in Surrey. The latter was where most of us went to die. He hadn't saved up a dime during his time in Hong Kong because no one did or could. But he had his little house on Lamma Island that he had bought early on but which he now hardly ever used. Perhaps he would die there, in sight of the South China Sea.

Twelve years ago the city had been a very different place, sheltered as it felt then from the storms of history. But the storm had returned and the long-established security in our hearts had vanished. Cunningham would continue writing stories about follies and outrages that even his own readers didn't care much about, and I, if I was lucky, would carry on living here doing reports for websites and agencies and occasionally magazines since I, too, had bought a little place for myself when the going had been good back in 2006. As long as you're not paying rent you can get by doing what you want—that had long been my philosophy.

One round later, willy-nilly, I paid for the drinks and went back outside to find a cab to take me up to the Mid-Levels and the Canossa Hospital, where I was well known for my minor accidents at parties and my mishaps at home caused by especially severe hangovers. That night, however, as I was slumped in the back seat looking out at the freeways turning circles within circles and the wet trees in the parks, inhaling traces of tear gas through an open window, it seemed to me that something had quietly come to an end. I had been assaulted by a local who had decided that I was the new enemy. In two decades of living there that had never happened before. The chemistry had changed, as it eventually does, and I was no longer invulnerable. We climbed above the city and were not far from where Jimmy kept his palatial apartment. The hospital was deserted and I was treated on the spot. A vicious wound, *la*—how did it happen? I lied because I thought it better to lie about what I now realized had been an ideological or even racial attack.

I walked down the hill afterward and heard chants and cries going up from the apartment complexes on all sides, as they did every night at the same time. Protestors not on the streets but in their own apartments, standing in the dark on their balconies and shouting encouragement to one another like the chorus of some enormous improvised Greek tragedy. Sometimes the playful English words "Add oil!" which had come to mean something like "Keep at it." I supposed that the Tang family, playing backgammon on their terrace every night, would hear these operatic cries as well and that Jimmy would like them more than his wife. But he would keep his mouth shut, even as he smiled inwardly. He was fond of quoting a piece of graffiti that had begun to appear on Hong Kong's walls: In the future, everyone will want to be anonymous for fifteen minutes.

THREE

TWO NIGHTS LATER, AS I TOOK THE ELEVATOR UP TO Duddell's, that discreetly elegant restaurant housed in an office building on the steep lane of the same name, and around the corner from Foxglove as it happened, I felt wet chills moving down my spine and the backs of my legs as the throbbing in my cheek grew worse. The wound had gotten infected in the bacterial heat. Yet the streets were clear. In the cab we had passed a lone tear gas canister sitting in the road spouting a plume of smoke like a little geyser. Nothing around it, just broken glass and pieces of fried rubber. It had strayed onto an irrelevant street by accident and no one had even noticed. Yet it had stung my eyes, and now as I reached the third floor and the club-like reception area of the restaurant my vision blurred and I had to ask the staff to find the table for me.

Jimmy and his guest were already there and, in a place famous for its wine, they had a bottle already in place that was worthy of Jimmy's exacting tastes. The woman glanced up and saw me first but without knowing who I was; a slightly quizzical disappointment crossed her face, but with a certainty that I was the one they were waiting for. She was self-contained in a way, neat long hair, and an asymmetrical face that would age in an interesting way. She was dressed in T-shirt and jeans but quietly on point; you would notice her even in passing. She said something to Jimmy and he half turned toward me. Dressed in a W. Bill summer suit and a white linen Calabrese scarf with paisley patterns, he had his back to the blind-dimmed windows, and as always he was a little too conspicuous. Obviously his guest was letting herself be plied with André Beaufort champagne.

"Oh, there you are," Jimmy said in Cantonese, confirming that impression. I saw that my place was already set, and as I moved to sit down a waiter materialized to fill my glass.

I said, "I definitely need that."

"Adrian, this is Rebecca. Rebecca, this is Adrian. Now we'll move to English because Adrian's Chinese is a bit iffy."

He was right, but it wasn't as if I couldn't hold a pretty decent conversation at speed. I shrugged at her and she seemed to understand that I was the shy sort and that she could cut me some slack.

"I thought you said he reads Chinese poetry."

As Jimmy winked at me her eyes fell upon me and something inside gave way, stepping backward into the wings and ceding territory. Her gaze had a shimmering heat. And so we switched to English, which was a shame, I thought in the moment, since Chinese might have suited our threesome better.

"Pleased to meet you," Rebecca said, shaking my hand. Her English appeared to be perfect.

From a good family, I thought to myself, and I knew the type. But which family? Jimmy used the city as his oyster without ever drawing attention to the fact. She went on, "What *is* that gash on your cheek?"

"Attacked by a bottle."

"A bottle? With a human attached to it?"

I told the story, wearily. Myself, bottle, lout—the whole sorry interaction. Jimmy found it coldly amusing.

"Sorry to hear it, comrade. Was there a war of words first?"

"None." I really didn't want to get into it, so I glossed over the exchange.

"Straight out of the blue, eh? If you want me to have him rubbed out just say the word."

"You'd never find him."

"Likely not." He grinned. "*La vie en merde,* but what can we do? Bear your scar like a warrior and make it a talking point with women, that's my advice."

For a moment, though, he looked concerned despite his flippant tone. It was on me, then, to put him back at ease.

"I'll live. Let's lose ourselves in food instead."

"The great pastime of the empty-headed. Which includes me, I'm happy to say."

"Order for me." I could always trust Jimmy's taste.

"Cod with peppercorn? Whelk with silky fowl and abalone?" His face was mildly flushed with anticipation. "What do you say, we're good for that, aren't we? Crispy suckling pig?"

He ordered in Cantonese. Rebecca slowly took me in with those same eyes that tracked small things as a matter of course. A stranger, not very attractive but full of empty words. The reverse of herself. The room was only half full and she seemed to fill it even with her subdued luminosity. She was one of those people who gives the impression of a physical stillness that is an accurate transcription of the internal kind.

I lifted the glass for a toast of some sort.

"Yum sing."

We drank together and Jimmy's eyes, bright and hard above the glass, found me and dared me to question his taste.

"Jimmy tells me you're a student," I began. It was a clumsy opener but someone had to start the ball rolling. She looked at him playfully.

"Is that what he said?"

"He's a terrible liar. Feel free to give me the truth."

"No, he's not lying—not now anyway."

"Calumnies," Jimmy protested. "She's a student at the university. We all were once. I don't hold it against her."

"I'm studying American literature."

"So how did you meet the great Jimmy Tang?" I said.

"On Tinder, obviously."

"Another lie," Jimmy protested again, but chuckling mostly for himself. "One should never divulge that kind of thing anyway. If you really want to know—"

"No," I said, "not at all. Like you say."

"—if you want to know," he persisted, "she's been pursuing *me* for years. I had to fend her off—but to no avail, as you can see."

I turned to her. "Is this true?"

She nodded, and right on cue, a plate of crispy suckling pig arrived looking as if it had just been flayed alive, with a side of jam and the cod alongside it. I understood something

then, just as Jimmy had said: that their families were connected, sharing habitudes of class and privilege. They were
poles apart on many levels, but at the same time literature,
money, and a shared social class in a small environment had
brought them together sufficiently to give life to a nascent
sexual spark.

Confirming this, she was soon describing her old school
in Switzerland. It was the École Chantemerle near Montreux.
Her father was a banker, a philanthropist well known in the
art world. A not-so-subtle hint was dropped that he and
Jimmy went way back. It was social incest.

That he had waylaid the daughter of one of his social
peers, if that was indeed what had happened, was not for
Jimmy the most salubrious decision. She spoke more slowly
than either of us, and once the school had been mentioned
she didn't seem keen to talk about herself much more. Nevertheless I could see ambition of a kind, a skepticism about
her own class that might have extended to Jimmy. Yet they
were playful and comfortable with each other. They had
shared a bed, I thought with annoyance. A reaction that was
surprising even to me. He had won her over in some way: the
liquid intelligence, the ability to quote reams of Chinese poetry from memory. To a young woman who shared those interests it appeared to be a combustible chemistry. And
perhaps very unusual, because in Jimmy's case it was fused
with glamour of a material kind. I could see it now. Few men
had those qualities nowadays.

"What about you?" she said to me.

"I'm a recovering hack. I've been recovering for a few
months—I probably won't recover at all—"

"Years, in fact," Jimmy interjected.

"—but now I seem to be healing. I write online dispatches for a news organization. It's owned by a billionaire in the States. It's nothing very serious. You know these billionaires."

She ignored that dig and when I mentioned the name she nodded but without much respect.

"You must be busy right now," she said.

"To tell you the truth, I'm running out of energy. I'm probably too cynical for this game. Running away from Raptors and all that. They can run faster than me anyway."

"They're getting faster, too."

Raptors, as the police arrest units were fondly called by their prey, were certainly quick. They must have been hired from amateur athletics teams. Jimmy made a quick face at me and—over a third pour of the Beaufort—I had to admit that I was reaching the time when one puts oneself out to pasture simply out of exasperation.

"You're twenty years too late, Adriano. But I admire you for going out anyway and fighting the good fight." He addressed his lover: "Our Adrian here thinks your generation are rather fine. He was a bit of an anarchist himself back when we were students, so I'm not entirely surprised. Not Kropotkin, but close. There was much talk of revolution on the lawns of the Cam."

"Is that true?" She turned to me with a sudden pulse of interest.

Kropotkin on the Cam, that had been me but only for about a year.

I protested, "He's exaggerating but not completely off. It was thirty percent Kropotkin and thirty percent Ruskin."

"He was confused," Jimmy said.

"Now I'm three percent Kropotkin and ninety-seven percent Mark Twain."

"Three percent Mark Twain."

She smiled. "I think it's generational," she said, putting down her fork and leaving the whelk on her plate untouched for a while. "I've had some pretty intense conversations with my father about it. My mother is beyond talking about it. We're not on speaking terms anymore."

"It's thousands of arguments over dinner tables every night," Jimmy said. "In my house it's just between me and my wife. She's more uncertain than she lets on. But her family can't afford a disloyalty scandal with regard to the Communist Party."

I was curious how Rebecca would react to mention of Jimmy's wife, but her face remained implacably neutral.

"She's just scared," I said. "Isn't everyone?"

"No. The twenty-year-olds aren't scared."

"That's because they're twenty. They have less to lose materially. They'll be scared when they're thirty. Don't you think so, Rebecca?"

She lifted her eyes to look at us for a moment and picked up her chopsticks again.

"Of course we're scared as well. You realize hundreds of us have been injured, don't you?"

"Obviously," Jimmy drawled, sounding like he'd heard this line before.

A crab dish had appeared laid out on a gold-plated vessel with two metallic claws. It was placed between us and Jimmy ordered another bottle to see it down. The abalone came, with flowers made out of vegetables.

"I'm afraid," Jimmy said, "that we've created a fair number of martyrs. Martyrs are very hard to dislodge from their pedestals. In the short term they'll be crushed. In the long term—the kids will grow up, they will inherit the place. Or is the plan to send millions into exile?"

"They'll just repress and do business with Silicon Valley as usual," Rebecca said without much anger. It was the way of this particular world, and there was unlikely to be a different outcome. "We're not doing it because we have any hopes that the rest of the world will lift a finger. We already know they won't. We're doing it because it's vile not to."

"You have to admire that," Jimmy said, meeting my eyes for a second, and almost with a regretful nostalgia just between us two. "Suicide theater. That's what I really think it is. Sorry to say so, Rebecca."

"You can think what you want. You'll regret it later."

The conversation about contemporary dramas was then put aside before things got fiery. I was fascinated by the golden claws and wondered out loud if they were brought out on demand.

"And you're still in that rat-infested place on Java Road?" Jimmy said. "What's it called?"

"The Garland. And it's not at all rat-infested."

"Roach-infested, then. It's infested with something non-human for sure. I should have visited you at some point, but honestly, I've always been afraid I might get bitten."

"Roaches don't bite." I appealed to Rebecca: "He's a terrible snob, that's all there is to it. He's not in touch with reality."

Jimmy brushed this off with a wave of the hand.

"I got him into the China Club and he's never forgiven me. Adrian, you should really find a rat-free apartment. The prices are going to plummet. Soon they'll be affordable even for journalists."

"Touché, but not for me. I don't get paid much, remember."

Rebecca turned to me with a smile that I thought wasn't wholly controlled, something inside her bristling with hostility.

"I didn't know journalists were starving. There are hundreds of you on every street corner. Where do you all come from? I would say it's a godsend: you get to cover a violent story without getting shot. It's a feeding frenzy. I don't mean to criticize you. If it wasn't for you—"

"We go where the stories are. We're mercenaries, obviously, and rather proud of it, too."

"That's the word. No interest in the cause—simply here for your own glory."

I said that wasn't quite true. In many cases, in fact, it wasn't true at all. Then I added, "But aren't mercenaries important sometimes? Every war needs them."

"Your days here won't last long, comrade," Jimmy intoned. "When they bring a curfew in, which they will, you'll all go home."

"Just wait and see," she said. "I think Jimmy will leave, too."

"Not me," Jimmy said. "I've got nowhere to go."

"What do you know about the curfew?" Rebecca asked Jimmy.

"I heard about it last night at a poker table. True story. The government minions are leaking it everywhere. Beijing gave the order, they say."

"When did they *not* give the orders?" Rebecca said.

Jimmy said, "They might not do it. After all, a curfew would be an incredibly stupid thing to do. And that," he sighed, "is why they will do it."

It seemed to me that something deflated in Rebecca. Her mood became listless, or just disinterested. We went upstairs afterward to the second-floor bar, which was more crowded than the restaurant. It was a hangout for the groomed and the rich: people with much to lose. There was an outdoor terrace filled to capacity with young locals in Armoury suits and drenched in humidity. I used to look at them with a measured envy, these beauties of the terrace, but now I just felt sorry for them. What future did they have in the new order that was coalescing around them? They'd still be rich, but they would be marooned as far as their other liberties went. They showed no signs of anxiety, however. It was a stifling night and the small-production gin flowed. We couldn't hear anything from the streets nearby. Queen's Road Central was silent, the Landmark was closed. The lanes that ran upward from Queen's Road were no longer thronged. The previous age had seemingly ended, and its more obvious street-level revels had finally dispersed. We went outside and Jimmy excused himself to go to the bathroom. When I was alone with

Rebecca, she turned to me and asked if it was true that I had once been married and that I had lost all my money gambling in Macao.

"Is that what he told you?"

She smiled behind a raised hand.

"He did. But perhaps he was pulling my leg."

He had been, so I resorted to irony. "No, it's all true. I had an illness and I had to lose all my money to find the cure."

The bright eyes revealed a moment's incredulity.

"And now you live in the Garland building?"

"I know you don't know it. But yes, I'm planning to die there, too. I can't think of anywhere better. Perhaps I'm a bit lazy by nature, or else we all are. We find a good spot and then we are loathe to leave it. It takes so much energy to get up and leave. Besides, I don't think I could adapt to a Western city now. London would be the end of me."

"It'll sound sad in the papers."

She said it in Chinese and I had to admit it sounded quite appealing. *London is the end of a returning Englishman.*

She went on, "So it's too late to go back to the UK? Many of us might be going there, as I'm sure you've heard."

"But for me home is here. I used to think one could pack up and leave toward the end of one's life. But it's not like that. Without knowing it, you cross a line and you wake up one day and find that it's too late to go back. But what *is* the line? I always used to think it would be my fiftieth birthday, and I crossed that line already. It's a sort of weariness. You think, 'What does it matter where I disappear? Hampstead or Mong Kok here in Hong Kong—what can it possibly matter?' And because you are in fact already in Mong Kok, or wherever it may be, you just coast along and die in Mong Kok. And no one is going to care where you died."

"Really?"

I shook my head, adding:

"Least of all me. I wouldn't want to die in Varanasi, for obvious reasons. But anywhere else—"

"But Varanasi would be the best place to die."

"You'd want to die alone, not surrounded by millions of other recently dead people."

"I think you just don't want to go back to your family. I understand that. Families are the worst, and I say that as a Chinese."

"May the gods strike you down."

After a beat I went on:

"You're right. It's sad, I agree. Families! I have a sister, a brother, and a mother, and really I should be taking care of them. But here I am being selfish. How about neither Varanasi nor Hampstead?"

She said, "I think I'd take Hampstead over Mong Kok. Not for living, but certainly for dying."

"You're not there yet. You're not even halfway there."

I felt myself flirting with her. Pointless obviously, but it was in some way from the heart. It had to be done with levity. Small talk swirled between us, she laughed once or twice, and we came, she and I, to a clearing in the forest.

"I hope you stay," she said lightly. "You don't have a girlfriend?"

I looked down at my fingernails and in that awkward moment they seemed even more ridiculous to me than they usually did. Untidy crescents, ruined by constant worrying.

"No. I've lost the touch for that sort of thing. I sometimes think it's because I've lost the knack for simple fun. *Fun* is the word I hate the most."

"Didn't Jimmy tell you one has to have fun before it all goes dark? I would have thought you were a fun expert. Aren't you?"

"Not at all, no. I'm a dreary person's dreary person."

But we were laughing it off, and she didn't believe a word of it.

"Jimmy and I beg to differ. With me it's a choice. I like coming over a bit dreary. It keeps the flies away."

"Ah." Of course I seriously doubted it.

"I think I might have to go soon," she said, stifling a yawn. "I'm actually quite tired. I inhaled too much tear gas earlier."

"What about Jimmy?"

"He'll go home to his wife and a hot toddy. It's a weekday."

"Simple as that?"

The eyes slackened a little, her uncommitted smile matched them.

"We go our separate ways. We're not tied to each other night and day, in case you hadn't noticed. Married men. I call them 'the tribe.'"

It was a step too far in the direction of confession and I could see that she instantly regretted it.

It's your game, I thought. Your rules.

She said, "You and Jimmy can stay out drinking, or whatever it is you two like to do. What a shame there aren't any opium houses left."

"Stay," I wanted to say. "The night is still middle-aged."

I then glanced down at her legs crossed at an angle to mine and noticed that there were spots of blue dye on her shins. The police used that dye in their water cannons so that anyone touched by their spray could be identified later.

"Where did you go?" I asked, in such a way that we both understood what I meant.

"Nowhere special—I wandered the streets. Who wants to know?"

"Didn't Jimmy tell you not to go?"

"He did but it's not his call. He can't go but I can. And since I must go, I do." She paused. "Same as you."

"Then I might see you out there one day. Don't be shy. You'll see me because I never wear a helmet."

"We cockroaches aren't shy—we're gregarious. I don't wear one either."

What I said next was almost serious:

"If we meet up like that I promise you I won't tell our mutual friend. You could even introduce me to your friends, if you felt like it. I'm curious about them."

"You mean 'the young,' as you call them? We're nothing special. We're just you without the experience. You weren't any different at our age."

I wondered if this was really true. In a single moment, provoked by such a comment, flashes of my past came back to me. Had I been no different from her, her generation, at that age? I couldn't answer the question. I said that sometimes I feel I was never young because increasingly I couldn't remember it. It felt like a pantomime I was acting in long ago. But I had lost the plot of it and now there was no plot at all. Growing old is never what you expect it to be. Beating one's oars, borne back ceaselessly into the past.

"Plot?" she said. "You're more sentimental than me. We're not a sentimental generation, if you didn't know that. We're spoiled brats but not sentimental spoiled brats."

"There's little wrong with being a bit sentimental. How can you not be?"

"But you," she went on, "had something to look forward to when you were young. You had a future. That's the difference."

It was the simple gravity of this commonplace that took me by surprise. Young people in the West were always talking like this, and they had been talking like this for centuries. Whereas in the end, in the real world, they always turned out to have a reasonably comfortable future. The Sex Pistols all made good for themselves apart from the odd overdose. "No future" turned out to be an empty refrain. Our rebels always eventually bought a ranch in Colorado or a beach house in Costa Rica. They were never in danger. But her generation in Hong Kong were facing a real future with no future, an actual oblivion enforced by banks, electronic warfare, and men with machine guns and telescopic sights. They were like the last pale flowers of Weimar. I thought then that if a human being takes on all the context in which she lives, it's also that context which makes them beautiful.

Jimmy reappeared then, still talking into his phone. There were always deals going on that no one else knew about— openings, business opportunities, ways to make money among his networks. He ended his conversation and affected a gaiety that presumably would last the whole night.

But he seemed annoyed when Rebecca announced that she was leaving. "Oh?" he said. "Did Adrian say something upsetting?"

"Not at all. He's behaving very sweetly."

He gave me an arch glance.

"He's white sugar, all right. And I'm going for a drink with him if you're going to be a dud."

"I'm tired of drinking," Rebecca said, meticulously folding her napkin back to its original square. "Take Adrian to Rōnin. You have a driver."

"The streets will be blocked," I said, hoping it would extinguish the idea since I, too, was growing tired of the endless drink in darkened rooms.

Jimmy threw up both hands in disgust.

"So now I have to go home?" he said petulantly.

"You can play Solitaire in your kitchen," I said. "It's larger than my apartment. And the house I grew up in."

But in the end she stayed, I don't know why. She must have been enjoying toying with us. Generations are usually at war but at the same time they often have a morbid curiosity about one another. We lay on the outdoor sofas while the stars seemed to be getting dimmer and smaller night by night. It was the effect of lachrymator and smoke rising into the atmosphere and forming a permanent shroud. Stellar insignificance. Crumpled and limp, their bodies had drifted together imperceptibly and now their intimacy revealed itself. I felt a curious resentment about it. Jimmy meanwhile complained about his in-laws, as Hong Kongers do, and falsely lamented his lack of acumen with money. *Lucre.* It slipped between his fingers, he said, and there was no helping him. He would end up one fine day in the Garland, just like me. Yet for myself I was thinking how, even now in our middle age, I couldn't compete with him, as I had known for a long time, and that between him and Rebecca there lay the warm exclusivity of Cantonese itself, that supple and mocking language which I loved to imitate from the outside, like a monkey doing simple math problems, but which I couldn't enter myself. So in another man's ancestral garden one plays the outsider, the half-idiot observer. In due course, however, distracted by my own sidelined condition, I found myself looking once again at the blue spots on Rebecca's legs and found that I could no longer recall when the police had started using that particular chemical. It was a new development, but it had arrived furtively. The strangeness in the way that ordinary day-to-day things became forgotten as if time itself had sped up. It made me think of a scene in the Chinese novel *The Three-Body Problem* in which an adult and a child are staring at the body of a slaughtered Red Guard and the child asks the adult if it's the corpse of an enemy or a hero. "Neither," the adult says. "It's history."

As we lay there mentally preparing to leave, a woman of Rebecca's age passed us, turned for a moment, and recognized Jimmy and Rebecca. There was a fussy greeting among the three of them and the newcomer, Kerry Hui, sat with us for a minute. She shook my hand and gave me an examining look. She was one of their circle, I assumed, a student like Rebecca in her final year, and they talked together in English as if I wasn't there, but as a courtesy to my presumed inability to understand Chinese. It was small talk, but there was a subtle tension underlying it, as if driven by matters mutually understood but not openly mentioned. Rebecca leaned to me eventually and said that her friend was an aspiring journalist and that perhaps I might be interested in sharing some advice with her.

The friend also moved closer and said, "I've read some of your pieces in *The Raven*. I think you have such a good style."

"Is that right?" I said.

"Yes. Can I give you my card? We could meet up if you don't mind. I'd be grateful."

I took the card, feeling excessively flattered, and Kerry got up almost in the same instant and announced that she had to leave. It was hard to get taxis home these days.

"Let's all go," Jimmy said, and gave me a sly look, as if I had found or made a fan. We went as a group to the elevators and the staff bowed to Jimmy more than to us. Rebecca and he were tipsily intimate.

Even as we were deposited on the street by the elevator, their banter in Cantonese had started up again. They were arm in arm already and I could see that they would not be going their separate ways after all. On Duddell Street there were dozens of small CCP red flags strewn over the wet sidewalks but only I seemed to notice them. Kerry kissed Rebecca, shook my and Jimmy's hands, and disappeared into the night. But as his car appeared Jimmy asked me if I wanted to come on a yacht trip with them the coming Sunday. It would be a tour of the islands with his own crew.

"It'll just be us three and the skipper. He doubles as barman. Makes a mean Bargirl. What do you say?"

I smiled. "There's no such drink as a Bargirl."

"Well spotted, comrade."

I couldn't think quickly enough to invent an excuse so I accepted on the spot and he nodded: a small triumph.

Rebecca shook my hand. The flash of friendliness from earlier in the evening reappeared, and was just as indecipherable as it had been then.

There is a saying often quoted in Chinese poetry, of which I was only ever a second-rate scholar, to the effect that a woman's beauty makes fish dive deeper and geese drop to the ground in shame. Like everything Chinese, it must have been based on centuries of empirical observation.

A moment later Jimmy announced that he had called a separate car for me as well, one of his three drivers always on hand.

"We'll see you on Sunday. Hopefully in a sailor outfit? If not—lederhosen?"

AS I WAS DRIVEN over to Java Road the chauffeur, in the Tang family livery, turned to me and said in Cantonese, "The city's one big traffic jam." The green arrow light suspended above the roads glowed and there was no sound of sirens, so I assumed that he was correct because the radio was also saying that the jams extended far ahead in the city. As we rolled to a stop he reached up and flicked on the car's interior light so that I could read if I wished to. There was a selection of newspapers that Jimmy kept at hand, as well as a bottle of Yamazaki single malt. Apparently there was a disturbance by Times Square and the traffic had backed up in all directions.

It was an opportunity to relish the fact that I had never been trapped in one of Jimmy's limousines before. As I was reading a paper version of *The Wall Street Journal,* a car pulled up next to us and I realized that there was no traffic coming in the opposite direction.

I looked up and saw a well-dressed couple who might also have come from Duddell's. All I saw was the nape of the woman's neck draped with a string of pearls and the man's hand laid across it. She glanced through the window at me and the smile was whimsically cynical. At that moment I felt airless and overheated, as if a toxic gas had swept across the congestion of cars, and I asked the driver if he could turn up the air-conditioning. But that wouldn't solve the problem of a thousand cars spewing their fumes into an enclosed space every passing second. It was fifteen minutes before the jam moved again. We came back out into the open air. Helicopters crossed the night sky, their searchlights blazing downward, and every few seconds the beams swept across the cars and lit up the faces caught inside them. All of us were now on stage, paralyzed by the lights, observed by a small audience suspended high in the air above us. Accordingly the panic went on inside me even as we emerged on the far side of the tunnel, and I wanted to motion to the woman in the pearls and the man caressing her neck as they moved off ahead of us. Though to say what? I was sweating and the wound on my cheek was somehow bleeding again. I thought only of one thing: escape and a hot shower at home. Return to privacy and invisibility. "It's a mess," the driver was saying, as if only to himself and not knowing how well I spoke his language. Winding slowly through the skyscrapers all the way to North Point, the buildings draped with now-sad Louis Vuitton models staring into space, we could hear chanting and drumming in the canyons around us, unseen but dominant. The only thing I now found comforting were the eternally decaying tenements harking back to the British days, with their vertical lines of air-conditioning units and laundry lines. It would take a tsunami to bring those down. It was, of course, because I lived in one of these myself, Garland House, built on Java Road in 1965, and I had lived there so long that the place felt as permanent to me as some ancient cave dwelling.

The driver left me there now, at the corner where my building rose above the Joy Foot Spa and a cut-price fashion store. The street was silent and deserted, as it never was usually. My building's striking yellow facade, only painted that color up to the fourth floor for some reason, looked quietly abandoned in the same way, as if all the tenants had left for the week or were surviving on canned tuna behind locked doors. The yellow pipes and valves that crisscrossed the building's front were filled with motionless birds who appeared to find comfort in the foot spa's red neon Chinese characters and the time-worn window blinds covered with images of sleeping beauties, their heads resting as they always do, on outstretched arms. That little image of a red-lit foot on the second floor had always been the sign that I was home. And so, tracing my usual exhausted steps, I went up to the fifth floor and let myself into the tiny warren of rooms now a single pocket of heat after four hours without air-conditioning. They were dark and musty by virtue of the drab wallpaper I had not roused myself to change in years.

Yet their patterns were filled with images of little birds and vines and I had grown used to them in the same way that I had gotten used to my routine-driven solitude passed in their company. I made myself a gin and tonic with piles of ice and turned on the TV. My hand appeared to be shaking.

I listened to the news as I did every night out of morbid curiosity, not believing a word of it. The pro-Beijing papers' coverage of that day's insurrections was as uninteresting as the previous day's, constantly downplaying the severity of events and minimizing their significance. It was to be expected. The ongoing charade, though, was always fascinating. And so after a half hour I retired to the laptop to get the real news. I continued drinking, slowly and with a certain consideration for myself, and I could hear above me the feet of Mrs. Lai traversing her floors in slippers while she shouted at her long-dead husband. A lone summer moth had found its way into the apartment and careened around the lampshades, yet I didn't have the energy to hunt it down.

By now I followed dozens of fellow reporters on Twitter, many of them locals armed with their own cameras who descended into the streets every day and followed events until the early hours of the morning. They had colorful handles: Hong Kong Hermit, W. B. Yeats, Flamethrower. During my weeks of wandering the streets with my own camera I had never run into a citizen journalist that I recognized. It was like a roving secret society using their phone cameras to document for the first time a slow-burn revolution on the ground. I had long realized that my own modus operandi and the publications I worked for had nothing to offer that could better these citizen reporters. We had been left behind. Like drowsy elephants we plodded after news that had long been divulged elsewhere at three times the speed. The only purpose we served was to bestow a sense of legitimacy to whatever items of information we saw fit to enshrine in print, even if it was only ever digital print. But it had become something of a con. We lied like everyone else. But we were absolutely certain that we didn't lie and we despised those whom we thought did.

The Chinese Communists at least understood that very clearly. Hence their contempt for journalism. I could never explain to them what the romance of it was. They had never seen *His Girl Friday*. Even if they had seen it, what sense would they ever make of it? But as for us, the dinosaurs of my generation, who among us didn't want to be Walter Burns buzzing amid the clacking machines of *The Morning Post*? As Jimmy had suggested, the once great romance of it was what made its current degradation so disillusioning. When I was forced to defend that same press to Jimmy's pro-Beijing friends, for example, I found myself sounding vague and uncertain about my own claims, my own purpose. "But Rachel Maddow and Brian Stelter are comical lunatics," they would say, looking at me with merry eyes and waiting calmly for some sort of rebuttal on my part, having of course no idea who Cary Grant had been. And what was I supposed to say? No they aren't and all is well with the Republic? From afar, in fact, I had watched the strange deterioration and debauching of the American media. It struck me that television journalists in particular no longer relayed anything of integrity. But print journalists were following the same downward trajectory as they sat under the tables of the powerful in Washington and sucked up the crumbs, the leaks from "unnamed sources" thrown to them by the intelligence agencies who actually ran the show. It was how they now monetized their product. I had lost count of the number of retired spooks manning the desks of CNN, MSNBC, and NBC and talking in place of journalists, setting the terms of discourse until the two groups were curiously indistinguishable. Very few talked disrespectfully of the national security state. None gave off any whiff of actual courage. The gap between ourselves and the Communists had narrowed and the journalist, after a period of being a romantic hero, had become what he had been all along, a hack, a hustler, and a propagandist. Of course, as I knew only too well, Walter Burns had been all of those things.

When dozens of protests erupted simultaneously across the city only the freelancers could be at all of them at the same time, each one covering a different scene in his or her own way. It was a daily collage that clunkier news organizations could not mimic and which rendered them largely useless when one needed to know what was happening hour by hour, or even minute by minute. Those twentysomething correspondents were the romantic heroes now, and their energies had relegated me in my own mind to a rather marginal position. You could argue that it was inevitable. In fact that's exactly what I would argue. But if that was the case I would soon have to find a new reason to carry on doing what I was doing. As Dr. Johnson once said, much journalism is little more than "writing on the backs of advertisements."

Strangely, these meditations didn't unnerve me at all. The overall mood of the city had an anesthetizing effect. Outside

it was still almost a hundred degrees. The air sour with hatred, the scream of far-off sirens multiplying. In the great
walls of tenement windows on the far side of the road I could
see faces massed behind the glass peering out tentatively as
the sidewalks emptied. I noticed that, for the first time in the
many years that I could remember, the clotheslines strung
outside those windows were now bare. They were not unlike
trees whose branches have been stripped of leaves by a passing tornado. Voices carried farther in the unoccupied canyons between the high buildings, sirens could be heard from
great distances, echoing endlessly, as if stabbing through a
tremendous vacuum, and all around there was a rippling
electricity in the airwaves; the herd spooked by the approach
of wolves who have not yet been seen but whose tremendous
and alien scent is on the wind.

FOUR

YOU LOOK AS IF YOU HAVEN'T SLEPT IN DAYS," JIMMY
said when we met three days later at the marina in Aberdeen.
It was where he kept the smaller of his two yachts, a Tecnomar motor launch inherited from his uncle called *Sweet Typhoon*. "Is that the case, comrade?"

"I've been sleeping nonstop since I last saw you."

"I'm relieved to hear it. You look like you don't get
enough sleep. I on the other hand get too much." He paused.
"We'll pick Rebecca up on the way. My skipper is ready. His
name is Tom. Well, it's not his actual name obviously but I
call him Tom. Everyone in the family calls him Tom."

"On the way where?"

We were already walking in hot sunshine toward the
gangplank, the elegant white hull of the Tecnomar and the
Chinese Tom all in whites with a brocade cap, standing there
watching the newcomer.

"Tom! Can we get this fool a screwdriver?"

"Yes, sir."

The skipper moved out of the light and into the interior of
walnut and brass where the bar was kept.

"What do you mean, where?" Jimmy said without looking at me.

As we climbed aboard he said that there didn't have to be a *where* on an outing like this, there had to be room for improvisation.

"We're going to pick up Rebecca on Cape D'Aguilar and then head out into the unknown. So many islands, so little time. We have lobster and Cantopop. It's a heady and slightly nauseating mixture."

Uninhabited islands: it was very much his style. The screwdrivers came when we were seated at the back with the fishing rods, shaded by an awning, and the iceboxes had been opened. They were filled with glass jars of black caviar and pots of crème fraîche. Tom put Wong Ka Kui on the sound system and we went out to sea away from the terrestrial heat and cement. I got through three screwdrivers and crackers with caviar. Soon we were skimming past the green fringes of Lamma and into a mild and pale sea populated with little islands whose names neither of us could remember. I knew Beaufort Island, however, and the Tai Tam Tau headland opposite it. We motored between them with the music blaring, turning toward Cape D'Aguilar and wild rocks agitated with surf. Its hillsides were carpeted with metallic jungle and bathed in sea mist, with the lighthouse at its summit lit by the sun. At a small bay called Hok Tsui Wan we threw anchor and waited for Rebecca to appear.

Sunbathing, drinking at a good pace, we looked down at pearl-spot chromis glittering in silent gangs while changing our drinks to hard martinis. It was Jimmy himself who now manned the bar, and he made his drinks recklessly strong. He danced as he mixed, moving from one espadrille to the other, as if his mind were elsewhere in place and time. The cove was sheltered from the wind that day and I could hear the cicadas rasping in the trees above us. It was enough at that moment to fill me with contentment; I didn't need to wonder what was inside Jimmy's mind. My own mind was confused enough. "There is no confusion like the confusion of a simple mind," as Fitzgerald once wrote, and that seemed to describe me perfectly in those moments. I was there, I supposed, to act as a buffer between them, to grease the wheels of their affair, to provide relief from awkwardness—it could have been any of these, or all of them, and it would all have amounted to the same marginality for myself. I didn't mind at all. One likes to be of service to a friend. And you need the moments when life comes to a standstill, becomes pure activity, and the unconscious climbs back into the driver's seat.

The sun was at eleven o'clock as I looked out over the bay. No one passed by here because the entire Aguilar headland was a marine science reserve owned by the Swire Group. There was a building for the scientists and nothing else, though visitors were in theory allowed into the reserve. It was bare under a blinding sun and its twisted vegetation did not move in the wind. To amuse himself, Jimmy threw down scraps of cured salmon to make curious damselfish come in closer, and while he was absorbed in this boyish task he asked me if I ever thought about retiring from journalism and taking up another profession. I said I would probably retire the following day if I could. He gave up on the fish, turned slowly on his back, and let the sun strike his oiled face, as if he needed it after a long period huddled in restaurants, bedrooms, and boardrooms.

"I could have gotten you into the real estate business, comrade. It's soulless but relatively easy. I still could if you need a new career. I have some beach houses in Shek O we could turn for a quick profit. People are trying to sell and move to the U.S. but all we have to do is wait a couple of years and the market will return. My father-in-law has the connections."

"Perhaps. It's tempting, even if I'm resigned to scribbling the rest of my days away."

"Are you? I'd say it was a shame, if you asked me. There's a million things you can do with your life other than that bullshit career."

I grimaced. "I'm well aware."

"But you don't dare to try something else. You're smarter than that, Adrian. You always had an A-one mind. Frankly, I was surprised you went into the media. It's a circus of minor talents."

"I had my reasons."

"Once, of course. But who am I to talk? I'm even more of a fuckup than you are. And more of a prisoner."

But his tone was level, studiously carefree, as if it didn't matter that much to him now. Yet he still felt the need to talk about it.

"I doubt it," I assured him. "In some ways neither of us is a prisoner. We've done quite well for ourselves. We didn't become translators, at least."

This was good for a shared chuckle.

"Thank God," he murmured. "Though I could have been the world's wealthiest translator. There's a thought."

"Yes," I conceded. "By the way, I wanted to ask you: Why are we meeting Rebecca all the way out here? You've already been seen together in town. Isn't it a bit late to be playing hide-and-seek?"

"Indeed it is. But all the same, it seems word was getting around a bit too much. I was a bit of a fool letting that happen. I thought Duddell's was usually quite discreet, as venues go. I was wrong, of course. Melissa has ears everywhere. You see how careless I am?"

But he was grinning in his insolent, childlike way—deep down it was all one big cosmic joke that only we were in on. And I did think of what Melissa had said to me privately.

He went on, "So I arranged for us to meet out here. I know it's a bit of a production. But what is life without a bit of maneuvering? I also wanted to get you out of the city for a day. You were looking decidedly pale last time I saw you. Unhealthy. You live like a vole. Kiss the sun, boy! Kiss it and make up."

I looked up at the island to our right, separated from the headland by a narrow channel, and as if reading my eyes Jimmy immediately said that it was called Kau Pei Chau and was uninhabited as far as he knew. Perhaps desperate fishermen had clung to it during the Song dynasty. Now it was a Crusoe island, marooned upon its waters. Our patter fell away and I shaded my eyes. The sun seemed to have produced a high-pitched whining inside my head, a tinnitus, and I caught the motion of languorous butterflies looping above the maquis. As I noticed their flash of gold and blue, I also caught the motion of something altogether more human. And indeed it was a man standing without much pretense to invisibility in the full sun, dressed in a windbreaker and a dark brown beanie. He held what looked like a camera with which he was shooting the winding lines of the rocky coast-line around us. A nature photographer, then? I wondered how he had gotten there. He couldn't have swum the thirty feet of the channel in a windbreaker, and if he had come on a dinghy it was nowhere in sight. I thought of calling out to him but he was so engrossed in his task, and so detached from us, that I thought better of it and told myself instead that it was probably one of the scientists from the Swire center who would not want to be disturbed. Curiously, Jimmy didn't see him at all. I rolled onto my back as well, slipped my sunglasses back on.

"Besides," Jimmy was saying, continuing the thread of our shared thought, "it's nothing to come out here—there's a free bus to Shek O. From there it's a two-kilometer walk or so. She told me she loves hiking out here. But in fact she could take a taxi all the way from the city. I told her to go to the radio transmitter up there and then just walk down here."

"Still, it's a palaver."

"If this got out it would be much more than 'a palaver.'"

For a while we fell silent. It was only gradually that I became aware that the man in the beanie had melted away and that he had been replaced by Rebecca herself. She had appeared on the road that ran alongside the cove on the head-land side, sauntering in the heat in a pale gray swimsuit with a small backpack hoisted onto her back. She must have

changed at the radio transmitter and then descended ready
for a short swim. I saw her first and for a few moments I kept
it to myself so that I could take her in; I was sure that she had
not seen me doing so, though of course she had spotted the
motor launch at once. I later found out that it was illegal to
anchor there, so either Jimmy had found a way to get around
the rules as he usually did or he had simply taken his chances
with being detected, prepared as he probably was to claim
ignorance of the law while administering a hefty bribe on the
spot. But as it happened, no one had noticed us; Rebecca had
come down quickly to the rocks and raised a hand to greet us.
She ventured onto the rough little gray beach just as Jimmy
snapped to attention with a burst of laughter and she waded
out until she was up to her waist. From there she kicked off
and swam toward us, reaching the boat with a few elegant
strokes. The ladder was already down and she pulled herself
up, not even slightly discomposed, refreshed by a warm and
shallow sea. Jimmy peeled the bag off her back, spun her
around to kiss her, and asked Tom to put up another parasol
on deck.

Jimmy winched up the anchor and the engines were
started. Rebecca shook my hand, and I thought her half-
serious, skeptical mood had in some way carried on effortlessly from the last time I had seen her. She knew how to
adjust to people, perhaps, and subtly so that the other people
didn't even notice. She looked as if she had taken some time
off from her politics, as if she had been sleeping in white
rooms with blue shutters in a different country and eating
nothing but butter and toast. There was a burnished glow to

her cheeks, and the drops of water on her skin dried almost immediately as the breeze hit them. She asked if Jimmy had gotten me drunk already, because it certainly looked like it.

"Me?"

"Yes, you. You look like you're as drunk as you can get and it's not even midday."

"Am I?" I said to Jimmy.

"You certainly are. You can't hold your martinis, comrade. You're a disgrace to MI6, or whoever it is you work for."

"I thought it was the Russians," Rebecca said.

"If only," I sighed.

"Was it a hellish taxi ride?" Jimmy said to her.

"I only came because you promised slipper lobsters. Can Tom make me a mai tai?"

"Tom, did you hear? The revolutionary wants a drink."

They were suddenly in each other's arms, but then they disengaged and Jimmy cried, "I'm putting on some French stuff. I'm in a Françoise Hardy mood."

He put on one of the songs from *Soleil*. It was "Mon monde n'est pas vrai." My world is not real. They seemed to know the words by heart, as if they had half-danced and canoodled to it many times before.

So, caught in this '60s mood, we moved slowly out into the open sea between Aguilar and Po Toi. In the galley Tom prepared the lunch of promised slipper lobsters, which had not yet been sacrificed for us. They were in a plastic bag dragged in the water by a rope, enjoying unbeknownst to themselves their last moments on earth. Around us in the dark blue marine universe other launches cut white trails as they made their way to equally secluded destinations. Wealthy part-time mariners fanning out in order to enjoy the privileges of solitude on the seas.

We moored along the volcanic rock coves of Beaufort Island. These other pleasure boats formed miniature floating domains from which people dived into the sea in snorkeling masks. We caught a few notes of their music and then they disappeared from view. Within a few nautical miles we were up against the pale brown granite formations of an island that, as we went around it, appeared to have no visitors.

ON THE ISLAND'S FAR SIDE the wind grew quiet and we dropped anchor in a channel that separated the larger island from a tiny insular outpost. Here, smooth boulders and outcrops lurked just beneath the surface as aquamarine shadows, and the rocks between the vegetation line and the granite masses were striated, polished, and inhospitable. Yet the sun made that same landscape glitter. On our platform we had lunch. Afterward, and now only slightly buzzed, Rebecca and I dived into the water and swam against the line of the rocks until we found other platforms among the formations. We hauled up and lay on the rock, chilled by the sea. On the motor launch held in place by its line, Jimmy, in white shorts, made insulting gestures at us with his hands.

"Is that sign language?" I said.

"It looks like it. He uses it when he wants to be funny."

"How on earth did he learn it?"

Then Jimmy called over:

"You look like seals—seals with brains and sunburn."

The music had changed. He had put on some Nana Mouskouri and he made Tom dance with him on the deck, hand in hand. It was possible that no one else in Hong Kong was listening to Nana Mouskouri at that moment and no one at all was dancing to "The White Rose of Athens."

"Really," I dared to ask her since we were alone, "how did you meet Jimmy? I don't really believe what he told me."

Of course I already knew their families were entwined, but I wanted to see what she would say in her turn.

"I didn't meet him at all. I've always known him. There was never a time when I *didn't* know him. He's a friend of the family. My parents would be horrified if they knew, more horrified than they already are by what I'm doing on the streets at night—that's why I had to come all the way out here by myself. You know how it works. Out in the open the press are everywhere so it's better to be safe."

"You mean out in the daylight?"

"Yes. It's better out here. At least we can breathe. You're going to ask me if I know his wife. I know you know her." She paused. "Is this awkward for you?"

"Awkward?"

"You go to their house for dinners, don't you?"

"It's nothing to do with me. Your business is your business. I don't talk to his wife about things like that anyway. Why would I?"

"Jimmy says you and Melissa are quite close in your way."

"I wouldn't say close." I tried to shrug as authoritatively

as I could muster. "We're social friends through Jimmy, that's all. His secrets are safe with me. I'm the Fort Knox of secrets. You're worrying about nothing."

She looked away, perhaps wondering to herself how true this was.

"I'm not worried about anything. Or if I am, I've got worse things to think about right now." A beat. "My father has already put a private eye on my trail. Did Jimmy tell you that?"

"How . . . melodramatic."

"The To family are all melodrama, trust me. My father is enjoying the whole thing hugely. I think he and my mother have a war room discussion about me every night; I wish I could be a fly on the wall. You'll meet them one day, I'm sure. They might even attend one of the Tangs' dinner parties that you like to frequent."

Leaning back on her elbows, she glanced up at the little festering wound on my cheek. She reached up and touched the wound with a single finger pad, exhibiting a detached curiosity, as if I had deliberately neglected to see a doctor.

"It looks quite distinguished. An honorable war wound."

She glanced over to see Jimmy still dancing hand in hand with Tom. She seemed indifferent to him at that moment. Instead of going back into the water we climbed a short way into the trees and into the din of insects, away from the master of the boat and his music. From a higher vantage point we were able to see Jimmy swimming around the anchor rope as if we didn't exist. This physical distance between him and us was novel, and I wondered if she liked it. It couldn't have been completely accidental. It must have been desired, even if only unconsciously. We stood still in the heat for a while as the salt water evaporated off our skin. She looked away from me resolutely, and this very gesture of evasion, determined by shyness, felt like its opposite. Vanity on my part, but I lapped it up in the moment. My skin began to prickle. I felt the air between us move with a very quiet energy. Sympathy, attraction on my part; curiosity, pity on hers. If only it was ten years ago and she was older, I thought. I was better suited to her than Jimmy, I carried on thinking. We both saw through him, but we couldn't see through each other.

She said, "He looks like a small child, doesn't he? Lost among his toys."

"If yachts are toys."

"What else are they? I think we're his toys, too."

"Well," I said, "that's because we like being his toys."

She admitted that this was true.

"Except that I'm not his toy," she went on.

"I've always wondered about myself. I can't say. If you're someone's toy do you always consciously know it?"

"He only *thinks* you're his toy. But you aren't really. That's what I like about you: you're not as sad as your close friends think you are. You stand up for yourself without anyone noticing."

Was that even possible? I thought.

I said, "That's a wild compliment."

When she finally did turn back to me, I thought that her eyes contained a glimmer of the thought I had had about things being different if we had met earlier. An impossibility, but not for the imagination. Either way, it was some time before we felt any necessity to go back down, and during that twenty-minute interval I felt heady with that very possibility, which wouldn't leave me alone. It isn't uncommon I suppose that a person meets the one they should have met years before, precisely when it's too late. We talked about her political activities at long last, though I didn't want to press her on them. The last thing she needed was an inquisition. She hated communism even though in her own way she was on the left. She had thrown herself into it not impetuously but coldly, as many of her friends at university had. They were galvanized by the Umbrella Movement back in 2014, which many of them felt had failed because they had been too polite and well-behaved. Now there was famous graffiti that proclaimed, addressing the Communist Party, "It was you who taught us that peaceful protest doesn't work." That was her worldview in a sentence. Violence was coming either way, and they would be the victims of it. To say "If we burn, you burn" was thrilling for the moment but it probably wasn't going to be true. They were going to burn and the government would not burn at all. It would thrive.

When we went back down, the water was darker and more tumultuous. A wind had picked up from the south. Back on the boat we resumed the daylong cocktail hour and lay around in the comatose state necessitated by the sun until Jimmy felt restless again and wanted to pull up anchor. He said he wanted to "roam about a bit" and sail around Waglan Lighthouse on the next island over. It must have been about three miles away. We didn't have any thoughts about it either way and so he decided for us. On the way we threw out baited lines from the deck, failing to catch anything, and I sensed Rebecca growing more distracted, just as she had at the meal at Duddell's. My questions had likely nettled her and then had driven her to reflect upon what she had said to me by way of answers. Was I an interloper from the wrong generation who shouldn't be trusted, even though she had said that she liked me?

WHEN WE HAD ROUNDED the southern tip of Waglan Island we cast anchor again and sat in the calm provided by the rocks. Under dark blue parasols we played cards and listened to classical Chinese music, bells and drums of the Tang. The mood had changed again, like something unexpectedly blown off course.

"Did you know," Jimmy said, "that if your penis curves more than thirty degrees when erect you might have Peyronie's disease? Have you ever experienced this, *tongzhi*?"

"Only when drinking tequila."

"Is that an advertisement for tequila? If it is, I want to try it. Can it go to forty degrees, do you think?"

Rebecca said, "You two have been talking like this for over twenty-five years, I can tell. Adrian, was he like this when he was twenty?"

"He was worse, much worse. But we did try to translate 'The Exile's Letter' together. It was a competition among the Chinese language students at the time. In the end we almost won the competition."

"The Li Bai poem?"

"Li Po, Li Bai. The very same," Jimmy said. "I know you know it. Every schoolchild knows it."

"We did study it at school."

"Like everyone. Anyway, Adrian and I translated 'The Exile's Letter' together at Cambridge in 1989. In my opinion it's the best translation since Ezra Pound's. It was even published in the varsity magazine."

"Is it online?"

"I very much doubt it. It's in print in someone's vault somewhere."

"So it's disappeared, too, then."

Jimmy turned to me with an exasperated look.

"It has not disappeared. It has just gone into hiding."

"Disappeared!" She laughed.

"You do realize that everything on the internet—I mean everything—will eventually disappear as well? People thought bound books would make them immortal. In reality it just gave them a two-hundred-year reprieve."

"Fifty-year reprieve," I said.

"Fifty, then. Or twenty."

But then, Jimmy went on, there was Li Bai, dead at sixty-one in the year 762. He had not disappeared in the end, because among other things he had written "The Exile's Letter."

"Did you know," Jimmy said, putting down his cards and retreating into his scholarly mode for a few minutes, "that his mother was an ethnic Turk? He was known for having foreign features. He wasn't Han. Yet he is now the quintessential Chinese poet. His name is on scores of Chinese brands. There is only one extant manuscript bearing his calligraphy. Chairman Mao used to own it: it was his favorite artifact from all of history. In the end he was forced to surrender it to a museum in Beijing. I've always wondered what it meant to

Mao, the man who destroyed monasteries and temples. What did he love about it?"

I said, "It was the impossible thought that you could actually touch the brushstrokes of Li Bai himself."

"Exactly. I think it fascinated Mao because he couldn't erase it along Marxist lines. The Tang era will always be with us, in our memories. Maybe that era was superior to ours. We have the five-mile suspension bridges; they have Li Bai. Some would say we'll all die long before getting close to that genius."

It was interesting to be talking about Mao on a luxury motor launch with slipper lobsters and martinis. But then, Mao loved dance parties and seducing young nurses—hundreds of them, according to some accounts. He was no puritan. The Chairman loomed above our pale blue skies as much as the ghost of Li Bai. Every age must summon forth its emperor. Jimmy said that in his view nations didn't change much over time. China was still an empire, just as the United States was and would always be an early nineteenth-century country, as Tocqueville had famously and cryptically remarked. Just as it could be argued that the English would always have a bit of the Tudors in them. Just as the French on some subconscious level would always inhabit the centralized land of the Sun King.

Jimmy recalled the terrible story of Mao's personal physician, Dr. Li Zhisui, who was summoned by the Politburo moments after Mao's death in 1976 to perform a mummification of the body so that millions could pay their respects to the Chairman publicly in the Great Hall of the People. Alarmed, Dr. Li had reluctantly agreed, even though he had no idea how to perform the necessary operation. But since the showing of the body would only be for two weeks he thought that it might be possible.

In a panic, nevertheless, he retreated to the capital's medical libraries in search of some guidance. If he failed to perform the operation successfully he would probably be shot. Finally he stumbled upon a formaldehyde procedure that he thought might work. It involved massive injections of the chemical into the Chairman's body, which they proceeded to perform. The cadaver immediately bloated up to an enormous size and the doctors were faced with a new dilemma. How could they make the body presentable to the public? Just at that nerve-racking moment the Politburo summoned Dr. Li a second time and told him that they had changed their minds. They didn't need Mao's body to be preserved for two weeks. No, they needed it preserved for all time. He was to proceed accordingly.

In the end a medical team was dispatched to Hanoi to study the mummy of Ho Chi Minh and were told privately that Uncle Ho's nose had fallen off and been replaced with a wax one. It was useful information. The same fate had befallen the mummies of Lenin and Stalin. Dr. Li returned anxiously to Beijing and set about making Mao materially indestructible. Dr. Li, that cultured and gentle man educated in the West, succeeded to the satisfaction of the Politburo and to the satisfaction of the millions of tourists who file past the crystal coffin between eight in the morning and midnight every day.

"But why," Jimmy went on, "do socialists have this obses-

sion with mummifying their leaders? I can understand the
Egyptians or the Incas. But Communists? It's disappearance
anxiety. They destroy the past and its culture and yet they
can't bring themselves to destroy their own cadavers. I can't
understand it."

"Yes you can," Rebecca said. "It's a result of hierarchy.
These are societies with emperors—it's all they know. Not
having an emperor is what is traumatic to them. Mao is just a
Napoleon. Similar height as well." She smiled into the sun.

"Everyone has emperors," I said. "From time to time
anyway. I wonder if they'll mummify one of ours."

"If you think you have emperors . . ." Jimmy sighed, pulling a mocking face. "You people—you have no idea. Our
emperors are *actual* emperors. When you write a tweet that
they don't like, you disappear."

"And you stay disappeared," Rebecca added grimly.

At about three the waves became choppy, signaling in
some meteorological way that our day was perhaps drawing
to a close and that we should think about returning to the
main island. The day was still clear, however. The delicate
skies of the early hours had not tarnished. Jimmy was in no
hurry either. We hauled anchor and motored across the open
waters toward Shek O, thinking to cast down there and
maybe go eat in one the beach restaurants. That secluded village was a place where many of the Hong Kong rich liked to
hide out for a few days and nights when they were tired of
the metropolis, and that included me.

Between forested capes there lay a small beach with a
semi-commercialized village behind it. Its alleys were

crowded with designer toy houses and old temples. There was a sloping headland immaculate with bare patches of granite while offshore dozed the pale shapes of islands.

Moored in the shallows I saw that the curious lifeguard towers on the beach were unoccupied. The lights of a restaurant called the Cococabana flickered into life. Whatever crowds had been there during the day had melted away and there was only a single man sitting on the sand playing a guitar. On a lone pole a digital clock displayed the time for nobody.

The plan was for Tom to drive the launch back to Aberdeen by himself while we swam ashore and then dried off in the dusky sun. The water came only to our chests in the event.

We sat on the sand for a while watching the sun and the launch turning as its motors revved. At this farthest outpost the city seemed to come to a standstill within an amphitheater of subtropical hills. A coolness sweeping down from the Dragon's Back mountain pass seemed to remind us of hunger. We dried in minutes and walked up to Cococabana. It was a modern cement affair with bossa nova playing through the speakers. There were a few upper-class bohemian customers from the village sitting at the outside tables. We sat there as well, shadowed partially by a tree wondrously taller than the restaurant, and the unspoken understandings among us slipped and slid until they finally became something new, an emotion triangular, three-sided, with myself as the shortest side and, otherwise put, Jimmy and Rebecca as the main stars on their little stage and myself as the audience.

———

WE HAD OUR APEROL spritzes while black kites circled the headland and then gradually faded from sight. Raw sea bream and marinated tuna on the plates, the candles guttering. Jimmy complained about the wine: "A French restaurant with the lowest alcohol taxes in the world and they can't even—" But I found I was in the middle of the brightest day of the decade, asking Rebecca questions that were, precisely because of their banality, a pleasure to ask.

"I'll go to grad school somewhere," she told me when I asked if she was thinking of pursuing an academic career. "Maybe the States, like everyone else. Do people here go anywhere else?" I said I didn't know. It was an escape from Hong Kong in any case. I watched her carve out an oyster with a little fork and I thought how remarkably adaptable she was relative to the man next to her. His moods came and went so fast that it was largely impossible to keep pace with them. She had evidently learned not to even try to keep up with his ever-changing states of mind. The cutting bitterness that sometimes surfaced in his speech was so alien to her that it ran off her without effect. Could she even feel it, or know what it was? It was a coldness out of the past, a disappointment in himself, of course. We were a curious generation. Lucky in so many ways because born into the prosperity of the 1960s but not as spoiled as the generations that had come after us; soft but not as soft as our successors. Our grandfathers had found us ridiculous. But beyond all this, it was Jimmy's doubtless inherited class that made him both sensitive and callous. Even as he teased her he was solicitous around her. You could tell that he respected her: when she spoke he listened carefully, limiting his own words. She was talking about her future career in the States. At one point Jimmy pointed out, "She's a wunderkind. But she won't boast about it because wunderkinds don't need to."

"I'm not a wunderkind. I don't even know what that is."

"It's a child who is kind and full of wonder. That's you. Adrian, I want to dance down there in the sand with the wunderkind. Would you be so kind as to hold the fort?"

Although it felt like mere minutes, an hour later I found myself looking down at Jimmy and Rebecca dancing barefoot in the sand. It was a ragged waltz set to the same bossa nova, and the other couples watched them with an envy tinged by their own regrets. I could tell that it was not the first time they had danced together. It might have been the hundredth time for all I knew. They danced like lovers attuned to each other's body. The wind whipped the loose sand around them and inspired by Aperol they moved back and forth, talking so quietly that I couldn't hear the words. It was like a movement that would never end of its own accord, something that would have to be stopped from the outside, bringing them back to earth.

FIVE

EVERY AFTERNOON THEREAFTER, FEELING SHAMED BY Rebecca's resolution, I ventured out with both a yellow helmet and an anti-gas mask which I hung from the back of my electric bike. Being cautious by nature I covered myself with press tags though these talismans only served, in the end, to attract abuse and aggression from a constabulary bristling with stun grenades and body armor. But for the moment, in the dog days of that fetid summer, I still held on to the illusion that they would protect me in the way of talismans or Thai Buddhist *sak yant* tattoos. No rubber bullet would sail my way; no lachrymator would be directed at me personally. I could move like a sacred person among the flayed and the flayers.

Initially at least, I thought that my tags gave me invisibility and I moved accordingly, with completely unearned confidence, through makeshift barricades and fires set by Molotov cocktails thrown outside police stations. It was a period of sacred madness. But soon it would come to an end. The order must have come from high up to give the scribblers a bit of rough stuff. Still, that week the streets still possessed their courtesies: free espressos and bottled water for passing mutineers, the crowds parting for ambulances, all the things that made their way into the international media and which set up an expectation of a mere family feud that would soon blow over. But the people far away in their democracies had little idea who they were dealing with and nor, for that matter, did I. That week I began to notice a hysteria creeping into the police as midnight approached on the weekend nights, the banging of batons against their shields like a Spartan phalanx, the surprise of tear gas canisters launched from the upper floors of tall buildings and overpasses, streaking toward us with plumes of smoke like failed fireworks and spinning with an antic malice toward our feet when they hit the ground.

Something in me turned but it must have happened more gradually than my conscious mind understood. It was like the nails of a steadfast building popping out one by one. The timbers move and shift, the beams quiver. On some weekend evenings there was a haze of fire and smoke in the wider streets of Central which helped the crowds there to feel the potency of their own numbers, the power of a formless mass directed against a single target. Everyone knew that their slogan was "Be water," a charming piece of advice from Bruce Lee concerning the evasion of an enemy's blows. But water can also be a punishing wave. Those human waves crashed against mainland banks, MTR stations, police stations, small deployments of cops which broke and retreated under a hail of missiles and then subsequently against water cannon trucks and sometimes against defiant taxi drivers who— a rare thing—detested them and plowed into them only to be stopped farther down the road, dragged out of the vehicle,

and beaten with staves. Everything was caught on cameras.
The acts of the citizen and those of the state. The umbrellas
that everyone carried—a symbol of earlier protests—served
many practical purposes as they were hung over security
cameras and used to shield faces from being identified later.
The great bristling machine of the Chinese security state had
been roused, and it was often foiled by the humble umbrella.

AT THE END OF the week I dressed up once again and went
to dinner at the China Club with my roving editor at *The
Raven*, Simon Strick, who was based in Singapore but came
over once a month to keep an eye on his contributors and
stringers. He was an American of about sixty who had
worked at *The Washington Post* in his younger years and was
serving out his crepuscular ones managing *The Raven*, a
widely read English-language online news site that he was
wearily unable to love despite it having hundreds of thousands of readers and having been a staple of the online news
environment for close to a decade. Something in him longed
for the days of clacking typewriters and tumblers of scotch.
He had grown fat in Singapore drinking his way through
upper-echelon whisky bars of the connoisseur variety (he
could rarely be dragged from the Auld Alliance) and eating
almost nightly at Odette. His clothes now rarely fit him. Yet
we both got our suits at W. W. Chan in Hong Kong, which
was how he also knew Jimmy, and he swore by the exact fit-
tings at Kevin Seah in Singapore. When I would go to meet
him at the China Club I would always find him alone by the
restaurant's top-floor windows with that disconsolate atmo-

sphere of men who are looking in life's rearview mirror while trying hard to keep their looks, which can only be done with clothes. But his suits, even though gleaming and well cut, were not flattering; his eyes explored every room for female attention but in return women looked right through him. Yet this dismal equation was not clear to him, as if in the end his fall from favor was a mystery. It was anything but.

At the same time he had done well for himself financially. Backed by a shady Singapore billionaire, *The Raven* paid far more than *The Washington Post*. He was on his phone when I came in and yet the jazz quartet playing in that Shanghai 1930s room must have made his conversation impossible. Maybe he was pretending.

"Adrian, I'm glad you're still breathing." He got up for a moment, a little unsteady from a few drinks, and shook my hand. "Lovely to see you, my lad. How are your lungs?"

"Broken."

"Ah yes, I can hear—you've gone downhill. And what on earth is that on your face? Is it infectious?"

"Oh, that." I reached up to it reflexively as I always seemed to do whenever it got mentioned. "I was stung by an insect on a hike."

"Were you, now? My god, the insects they have here."

He was earnest as he patted my shoulder. "Peking duck all right?"

"Why not."

He went on, "I'm staying at the Icon. It's a hell of a place, completely empty. You can see all the riots from there. Maybe we should run a piece about hotel occupancy rates?"

"Don't ask me to write that one."

He grinned and the teeth were an artificial off-white but uniform all the same. It was insincere dentistry to say the least.

"We do have to capture the whole picture in some way, Adrian. Not that we don't appreciate your street coverage. It's exceptional. But it did occur to me that down the line you might be putting yourself at risk there and we do have to think about medical costs if you get properly fucked up. There are bigger insects out there, I'm sure. On the other hand, I personally would like to see some stories about the hospitals. Can't you get inside one?"

"No interest in that, sorry."

"The thing is, everyone else is covering the protests. You've done some sterling work, of course, and it's the story of the moment, but is it entirely ours?"

"I'm trying. But I never seem to quite catch it."

"I didn't want to be the one who said it. I do know what you mean. It's like running to the scene of a crime and catching a pair of coattails whipping around the corner just ahead of you."

I laughed. "You've nailed me there. I'm not fast enough anymore."

"Better to do something deeper and at a slower pace. Don't you agree?"

I could feel his grip tightening. "I've nothing against it."

A moment later I found myself looking across the room in expectation of encountering someone I knew, the half-forgotten faces that sometimes come back to you in a restaurant's rush hour. At the club it was not unlikely. Under the black lacquer fans everyone looked slightly familiar, as if I had met all of them at least once before without remembering any of them consciously. But at the far end of the room, besides a wall covered with Chinese calligraphy, that same eye caught sight of Rebecca eating with what looked like her parents at a table by themselves. They were all three dressed in white like people at a garden party—or a religious ceremony—even though it was by then past nine. While her parents, if that's who they were, had their backs to me, Rebecca was facing me. I seemed to recall something Jimmy had said about her parents being members of the club.

This apparition served as an improvised inspiration and I said, not taking my eyes off her, that maybe I should write something about upper-class families and their children who were taking to the streets.

"That's a splendid idea," he cried.

"Could we do it?"

"Of course we could do it. I think it would be immensely interesting. Gripping. Involving. I mean, what is going on with them?"

He knew perfectly well that I had a foot in that world and could likely write about it with some confidence. But discretion would be another matter.

"Would you consider it?" he asked.

I said I would think about it, that I didn't want to ruin people just for the sake of journalistic voyeurism.

"Would it ruin anyone?" he asked, eyes opened to express his full incredulity.

"You know perfectly well it might."

"I didn't say expose their secrets. I would just ask them their opinions. On the record. They wouldn't do that?"

"To be honest, I have no idea."

"Well, we wouldn't be trying to humiliate anyone. I don't want any lawsuits. But on the other hand we all know how it works. It's our job to get to the bottom of things. We can't do that without offending anyone."

"But must we offend my friends?"

He chuckled and his eyes revealed just how much he was enjoying needling me.

"But we're always trying to do that, aren't we? Offend your friends. Who are your real friends anyway? Let's be honest. We both know that the story counts for more than loyalties. Personally, I would love a piece on your friend Jimmy Tang. You'll never write it, of course. Because you're loyal to him and you know what it involves . . . But seriously, think of what a succulent piece it would be. Think of the hits we'd get inside Hong Kong. But go deep, can you? Dredge up some outrageous stuff. Then we can talk."

At this moment I looked up again at Rebecca and her parents and almost immediately lost interest in what Strick was saying. I considered getting up with a good excuse and walking over to their table. I wanted to know what her parents were like, the people who had produced her. Her father turned his face toward the rest of the room and I got a good look at him: a grave-looking and handsome man with facial furrows that indicated not anxiety but a relaxed ease with the conditions of his world, or even a mastery of them. But Strick was talking money and I couldn't extract myself. I nodded, barely listening, and immersed myself in the far-off table. Soon, as if attuned to my distraction, Rebecca got up and her parents slowly did the same. The mother turned and I saw that her face was an older version of her daughter's, except that her nose had a more imperious rise. They had finished their meal and made their way with satisfaction to the door. Seizing the moment, I made my call-of-nature excuse to Strick and threaded my way through the maze of tables to the same door. Within five steps my heart was beating out of sync with my mind, and when I got to the door and asked casually where Mr. and Mrs. To had gone, since it was a certainty that the staff knew them, they said the family had retired to the bar upstairs. I looked back at Strick, now returned to the intrigues of his Galaxy phone, and decided to make a quick dash to the bar to see if I could find Rebecca and her parents.

The Long March Bar was as full as the restaurant, as if the China Club served as a collective memory of better times. The bar itself was a homage to the 1930s, with its velvet armchairs covered with what looked like lace antimacassars and its poster art celebrating the Long March. Communist heroes standing on prows, gazing into future horizons that never came closer. Its iconography always reminded me of the artist who was beaten up by the Red Guards for depicting Mao standing at the edge of a cliff, thus inadvertently suggesting that the Chairman had lost his way. Steel ice buckets and stained-glass windows, images of Mao's missile force and old-fashioned silver ashtrays. Long and narrow, a little tongue in cheek, it was lit by gold-colored lampshades. And it was only at the last moment before giving up that I spotted Rebecca seated alone at the bar's far end, disburdened of her parents. She was not slumped in a sullen and resigned way, but instead simmered (as I thought) with resistance to every-thing around her. I looked around for her mother and father, and after a moment had passed I felt sure that they had in fact left the club altogether. If they had, I was alone with her.

I walked down alongside the bar. Past the bulbous backs of the businessmen in their black suits, past the foreigners slouched in the green armchairs with ornamental lace cover-ings, until I was level with her left shoulder and she was forced into awareness of a stranger at hand. She turned and at first didn't recognize me, or at least I thought she didn't. She had been reading a small book that I now saw was splayed on the bar in front of her. The interruption might have been unwelcome, I couldn't say. Two seconds separated my "Hi" and her formulaic smile. What a coincidence, she said. Was this somewhere I came frequently?

"Only on full moons. Are your parents members?"

"Since the old days. But Jimmy said you were a member here, too?"

"I'm here on a platonic date."

"Oh?"

I was quick to describe Strick.

"Is he waiting for you downstairs?"

I waved a hand. "He knows how to amuse himself."

I asked if she was alone and she shrugged, as if to say, What of it? But then: "No, I was having dinner with my par-ents."

"Mind if I sit here?"

"You can sit anywhere you like."

I had noticed the seat on her far side, the last free seat at the bar, and had made a preemptive move toward it when I saw her eyes object. It was as if her mother might show up at any moment.

"They'll be fine without you," I reassured her with a wink.

"My mother and father? I'm not worried about them."

Then I thought that perhaps it had been a reflex in regard to our absent mutual friend.

"They looked quite content," I went on.

I suppose they're not much older than me, I thought grimly. The same disconsolate niche.

"Let me get the drinks. Gimlets?"

"Oh God, no."

"*Yee loeng bu gimlet,*" I said to the barman.

"I'm doomed."

She groaned and swayed, conceding.

I asked if her parents would smell her breath after she'd been out at night.

"They would if I let them."

I glanced at my watch and realized that I had by now left Strick alone for the better part of a quarter hour. He must have made inquiries about me. But if I went back down to the restaurant to look for him I would almost certainly lose my interval of solitude with Rebecca. I decided against it.

I would leave a message for him later explaining that I had felt ill and had gone home without telling him. I hoped that he wouldn't take the initiative and come up to the bar to look for me. It was perilous since I depended on him for my monthly paychecks, but there are times when practicalities don't matter. Rebecca and I drank our gimlets and ordered two more. I noticed then that she was wearing the kind of lipstick that did not come off on the rim of her glass.

"I was never much of a drinker, even if you thought otherwise. In fact, I kind of hate it."

"You do?"

"It's a habit." She paused thoughtfully. "Why do we have all these pointless habits?"

We touched glasses and the steely gin hit the nose.

"Beats me," I said. "Because it's easy?"

"It's like you living at the Garland—you must like it *because* it's a habit. It's like what you were saying last time about getting used to a certain way of life."

I said it was like an old armchair you can't stop sitting in. It was like some old theaters in Hong Kong that one couldn't resist wandering into just to find a long-gone age. Like the Sunbeam Theatre near me, which played Cantonese opera on Sunday evenings.

"You know the Sunbeam?" she said, and I was sure she was charmed a little. "My parents used to take me there when I was little."

"It's around the corner from me on King's Road."

"I know where it is, Adrian. I love that you know it. Are you a Cantonese opera fan?"

"I like the ghosts."

"Doesn't everyone?"

She put both hands on the bar, the left covered with three rings, the right with the nails painted a dark scarlet.

"What about your friend downstairs?" she said.

"He'll live. He probably went home already. Should I go down and check?"

"No, because then you won't come back."

"Do you want me to come back?"

"Why wouldn't I?"

I said that was for her to say. Then I added: "What about Jimmy?"

"What about him? He didn't call tonight. He's not my boyfriend in case you thought he was. He couldn't be. He's my pass time."

I laughed. "Was that it, then?"

"You know what Indians call doing nothing? Doing pass time."

"You knew they'd have a word for it!"

"It's not the same as doing nothing, see."

She looked at me sarcastically, then said, "Jimmy, you know, he's fond of you, in his twisted way. He *is* twisted, and you know he is. If you made a pass at me he would probably have you fed to the pigs. Or the goldfish."

Too old, I was thinking already, this is not your game, Adrian, and you cannot win at it. It's just an amusement, especially for her.

I said, "Maybe we shouldn't talk about Jimmy."

"I hate talking about him, too. I like talking *with* him but I hate talking *about* him. About you as well."

"Do you ever do that—talk about me?"

She was too quick to argue and said that no, they didn't. She hadn't meant it. But of course she did.

"The thing that baffles me," I said, "is why you would hang out with men our age. I really don't understand it. You have beautiful boys your own age."

"Jimmy is fifty. You're about the same, I assume. In Hong Kong it's an unremarkable difference. We're not as neurotic about it as you Westerners are. Until you brought it up, in fact, I hadn't thought about it that much."

"Then I'm sorry I did. It was sort of stupid, wasn't it?"

"You know better than that, you've lived here a long time. But you're forgiven. You're both young-looking for your age anyway."

Then I asked her what she thought about getting out of the China Club and going for a walk. It was exquisitely dangerous to walk around at night now, in a suit and tie, in a real dress, dolled up for an opera that was no longer being performed.

She said it was by far the best idea of the evening. I said that we could walk through Chater Garden next door if she liked—it was relatively calm tonight. We could walk off the coming hangover.

"From two gimlets?"

"You're the lightweight."

In the space of a moment she had become charmed, though not, I surmised, by me.

WE WENT DOWN TO the vestibule, a de facto gallery of Chinese artists whose works cover the walls, and I peered into the restaurant to see where Strick was. He had stayed on with his bottle, chatting to people at a neighboring table whom he evidently knew. While Rebecca and I were waiting for the elevator I asked one of the staff to wait five minutes after we had left and then approach Strick with an explanation for my absence. I had felt sick and decided to go home. I slipped the boy a tip, in the old-fashioned way.

We went down alone in the elevator, awkward for the first time, and out onto Des Voeux between the Bank of China's two stone lions. The road with its curving tram lines lay empty under the overwhelming presence of the HSBC Building and on the far side of it Chater Garden's still-summery trees basked in orange light. We crossed over to the neoclassical court buildings and dived into the gardens fringed with Chinese fan palms.

The long L-shaped pool there was covered with dried leaves, as if it hadn't been swept clean in years, and the paths were bathed in the massive light displays of the towers around it. The other, newer Bank of China building, with zigzagging white neons alternating rhythmically, and the HSBC Building nearby projecting immense red and white graphics of bamboo leaves into the surrounding darkness. I didn't know why I had asked her for a walk in the gardens, the decision had not been entirely conscious. A small park which would probably be quiet while the cop vans were spread out along Chater Road. I had seen their flashing lights earlier and, sure enough, they were still there when we came down. On Des Voeux Road, in fact, curious impromptu barricades of uprooted potted palms lay unmanned among trash bags and sundry debris designed to deter traffic—succeeding almost completely. Only a few teenagers in gas masks, holding their signature umbrellas, slipped by in the quiet. In the gardens the rubber trees brought in by the British long ago dripped with a multitude of aerial roots and in the middle of the paths Chinese holly trees cast a sticky gloom down onto our heads as we passed underneath them.

Rebecca explained that she and Jimmy would sometimes go to a house that her family owned on the Peak, a small mansion that her father had built in the 1980s for his own use, but which he had given to her to use as a pied-à-terre. A place above the city in the green hills to find a little peace. Her father, she told me, had used it for secretive poker parties before the Handover. After that he had gradually abandoned the place to his mistresses, and when they faded away he had given it to her. Now she and Jimmy sometimes met there to be alone. But somehow I couldn't quite imagine it. I was probably just a touch jealous. We walked on the flagged paths at a slow pace, a few inches apart, and I could detect the perspiration on the back of her neck. There was something about it that reminded me of a pleasure that was once familiar but which is now faded and lives only in memory. Meanwhile she had launched into a description of her family and their anxious disapproval of her political activities. It would have been surprising if they had not disapproved, being an old and respectable family. The risks to both Rebecca and them were enormous and the outcome was bound to be ignominious for the family. She said that her father lectured her about it; her mother had sunk into exasperated resignation. They understood the issues abstractly, of course, but they could not accept her course of action. And so parents and child had reached an impasse.

"Personally, I don't care that much," Rebecca said. "The

city is over and done with if you ask me. It's disappearing around us. In ten years' time it will be unrecognizable. Just another anonymous Chinese city."

I said it was bound to be so.

"I'll be a janitor by then."

She shot me an unconvinced look, then smiled. "You'd make a fine janitor. Me, I'll be in Canada, or somewhere equally safe and bland."

I said that was the saddest part about it: the departure of her generation. A new wandering diaspora would be created. "It would be ironic if you left and I stayed," I said.

She seemed not to hear me, her shoulders now moving through spots of shadow and light, her sweat made even more noticeable by the heat. Her arm slung by her side glittered with a lone watch strap.

"But maybe this city was just a hallucination after all." She made a quick survey of the towering neons around us as if to make a gestural point. "It was never meant to last. I wonder if I'll come back when I'm old and remember you and Jimmy. Light joss sticks for you both."

"Please do. As spirits, we'll appreciate it."

"You'd do the same for me, wouldn't you?"

"I've got at least twenty-five years on you. It's not going to happen."

You never know, her face seemed to say. We let the matter drop and continued walking, in that way people have when they know that the unspoken is far more interesting than the inverse. Yet it was a small park and soon, if you weren't careful, you'd find yourself doing laps. We came to the end of the promenade, and the issue arose of going our separate ways.

"I'm going up to the Peak now," she said. "I suppose you must be busy, too. Jimmy's staying in town tonight. He has some engagement with his family. So I'll spend a night up on the mountain. I like it much better up there."

I said, quite spontaneously, that if she liked I could take her back in a car and then have it drive me home afterward. It was a small detour.

"You don't have to do that."

"It's a gentleman's duty."

She seemed to be made pensive by the idea of gentlemen and their duties.

In the end it was a short drive at night and there was no reason for her to say no. The roads were empty on the way up the mountain, twisting through moonlight dispersed through leaves, and the Peak's vertiginous jungle was bathed in the light of arc lamps. She rolled down the window and slumped against the clammy leather of the seat. I wondered if she was bored by me. She didn't say so at least and, as before, we didn't need to talk anymore. That was refreshing. The less you talk, the more you feel. The more you feel, the less there is to say. Eventually the driver left us at the tram terminus and I asked him to wait for me while in the dark Rebecca and I walked up to Lugard Road, a three-mile pedestrian walkway with iron rails built by the British in 1914 that cuts through forest as it circumnavigates the Peak. It winds its way past steep jungles of machilus and camphor trees, past views of a city that from this height appeared at that moment submerged in its own distant light.

The path by now was deserted. But from the city we could hear the dull thudding of police helicopters invisible in the skies. I had never imagined that anyone could actually live on Lugard Road but now that I was there at night I noticed structures that I had not registered before. Both above and below the alley stood immense and gloomy villas from a by-gone age, some with grandiose terraces lined with columns. Most appeared deserted and in a state of semi-ruin. Looking up from the road I could see the windows of rooms whose ceilings had been stripped bare to reveal the insulation and rafters. A few were still occupied, by people so rich that the adjective itself was meaningless. They must have been the most expensive houses on earth. One uninhabited house below the road possessed a palatial greenhouse whose panes were stained with moss and, next to it, a covered walkway connecting it to the house. It was impossible to know who had once lived there or who still held this parcel of land worth tens or even hundreds of millions. The great families within these houses once intermingled with the ghosts of my own nation, who had retreated here to escape the heat, bringing with them the comforting flora of India and Malaya. Their weeping Indian rubber trees draped roots over the road and brushed our faces as we went underneath them. There were steep canyons of Livistona fan palms humming with night insects, and perched above rock walls loomed her grandfa-ther's house, topped with barbed-wire fortifications and iron spears. There was no visible clue that we were near any kind of city. We approached it by a ramp protected by grilled gates that seemed to have been disused for a half-century. As we drew near, two ancient wall-mounted lamps came alive auto-matically. At the gate, she held out a hand and shook mine, and the exchange was not quite as warm as it could have been. She was self-conscious, I thought, but the same was as true of myself. I told her that we'd be with Jimmy again within a week and until then maybe it would be a good idea if she stayed up there on the Peak among the Livistonas and out of trouble.

"I could say the same to you, Adrian. You should go back to restaurant reviews."

"I was a terrible food critic."

"Thank God for that. Now that you mention it, staying up here is not such a bad idea, after all. Don't you love the smell up here?"

"Jungle," I breathed.

"How could one live in a place without jungle?"

It would be like being dead, I thought.

And it was then that I noticed something jarring. The lamps cast my own shadow around me, throwing it up against a wall for a moment and along the pavement. One notices such things on a lonely walk. Within a tunnel of shadows, I thought, your own becomes more noticeable. But when I glanced down at this moving shadow-show set in motion by my walking, I thought for a moment that I did not see hers. Even when the lamps were almost above us and a sharp shadow flowed out from my feet, I saw none emanating from hers. It was as if the light bounced off her in a different way or passed right through her with no effect, or else it could easily have been the interplay of light and shadow at that hour of the evening. In any case it was time for farewells. She turned and buzzed herself in and the lamps went off, moving into the darkness. A rectangle of lunar light flashed across her back and I wanted to say something light and witty yet somehow true that could be tossed after her. But the words didn't come to me. Such moments come out of nowhere, fast as curveballs, and usually they aren't seized. I turned.

On the way back down from the Peak in the same car, the driver peering at me in the mirror as if I had failed some erotic assignment, I thought over how even now I had still not even remotely tackled the riddle of Rebecca To. I felt that something had been held out to me—an offer of some kind— but that at the same time it was nothing at all, just a passing mood late at night. In reality she had probably not even noticed the alterations going on in my mind because they had nothing to do with her, strobe-like as they passed through me, and afterward I was not sure whether anything about them was real at all.

SIX

WHEN I GOT BACK TO NORTH POINT THE STAIRWELL at the Garland was filled with an aroma of steaming sea bass and chives, and the walls were clammy as if they had turned into something organic and begun to sweat. From inside the units came bursts of martial music mixed with Mandarin variety TV shows. It was as if they had all turned up the volume of their sets to block out the exterior world. As I fumbled for my keys I sensed an eye tracking me from inside one of those doors. The *gwailo*, the white ghost, as they called me, was home and he had not been home all evening. Instinctively I locked the door from within with both security chains, which I never normally did, and took a bath with the help of a bottle of rum.

Even in my bath, however, I could still hear the demented TV sets. Something had set them off, in the way that crows or dogs are set off. The tenants were stirred. I found to my surprise that it was the first time I had ever noticed. I didn't know them and obviously they didn't know me. We all knew that we might be spied on by tenants hired by the security services. The walls were little more than paper; any ear pressed to them would be as effective as a bug. After all, I myself could hear the strains of the TV series *Wo men de si shi nian* in the room next to mine, and I had no idea who was in that unit. I was half-sure that I had seen an old lady standing by its door one day with her keys. But it had been long ago. Yes, it was certainly *Forty Years We Walked*. I had watched it once on a flight to Xi'an. It made me smile to hear it through a wall now. But at the same time it did not feel as coincidental as it should have felt. It felt as if it were directed at me specifically.

Still in the bath, I called my jilted editor at his hotel and apologized for my disappearance. A sudden attack of nausea, I explained, coupled with an inexplicable weakness in the legs—all the recent stress had been getting to me.

"You're full of shit," Strick said. "I saw you with a girl. But we'll let it go this time. I was just about to call you, actually: I need you to go to the hospital where they're holding the kid who was shot tonight."

I'd heard nothing about a kid being shot, but then I had heard nothing about anything since the afternoon.

"You know which one?" Strick asked.

"I'll get on it right now, maestro."

"Good lad. And try and get him to be distraught on camera."

"What?"

"Distraught, Adrian, distraught. I don't mean *make* him distraught. I mean catch it for the world to see."

I looked up the incident on Twitter and found the hospital in Mong Kok. A sixteen-year-old had been shot by a Raptor on a main street in view of dozens of journalists only four hours earlier. The story was already out. But I was not being dispatched to the hospital in order to obtain a scoop. I was going there to provide a segment of emotion for our readers. Drowsy from the rum and the hot bath, I decided to wait until the following evening, however much the delay would annoy Strick. Still, I made my own hours.

The next night, I walked over to Fung Shing first and burned through a plate of steamed bean curd rolls. The place was crowded with now-boisterous—perhaps emboldened—men with fresh haircuts, and I got a few stares as if they had mentally formed a mob, though I was too starved to care much. In any case, from there I taxied across to Kwong Wah Hospital in Mong Kok, that replica of a Knights Hospitaller fortress that rises up on Dundas Street. There was a crowd in the foyer and out on the street so I had to flash my press card several times to get inside. The injured boy was in a private room and visitors were almost completely excluded. It had been an unusual incident, since weapons were not readily used on either side. I gathered that a cop had lost his temper during a brawl and let off three shots at his antagonists, of which one was this boy. It wouldn't make world headlines but all the same a few policemen without their gear were there to gently push us back and, I assume, quieten us down. They seemed to have been ordered to calm the situation down rather than the reverse. Hong Kong was a city where shootings were largely confined to the underworld realm of gangsters. Now it was happening to students.

On the steps outside, in the sordid melee of the frustrated press, I ran into Cunningham, who was there for an Australian channel. He was dressed in a seersucker jacket that had wilted around him. He pulled me aside from the fray and told me that the kid wasn't going to die but that his family had put out a statement that they were going to sue the cops. It wouldn't go anywhere, of course. Suing the police had become an improbable venture under the new dispensation.

"Did Strick send you down here?"

"Who else?"

"There's not much of a story for you now, old boy. You're too late." He gave me a consoling smile. "I see your face hasn't healed."

I hadn't thought about my wound for quite some time, but now that I did—courtesy of this observant clown—I felt it itch again and gave it a feel with my hand.

"Oh, that," I muttered.

"Looks like it got infected again. You have to be careful with nasty cuts like that, Gyle, like I said last time."

He smiled and I was supposed to take it as a caring reproach.

I said, "I've been too busy. Look, Cunny, if everyone else has already got the story we might as well sod off, right?"

He sighed: "Not me, I have to stay. Editor insists."

"All night?"

He glanced at his watch, as if it made a difference.

"As long as it takes. I know it's pointless."

"Where's your cameraman?"

"He's taking a piss inside."

"Well, I feel like I'm at the back of the line here. It's like half-time at a rugger match."

But all the same I sifted through the crowd of journos who were assembled with us and I could sense that they were waiting for updates that would be worth something in their newsrooms. It was a mood I was long familiar with. The gathering of our guild in a single place in search of a story we all wanted, the rivalries mellowed by a shared futility. The wisecracking camaraderie getting drier, more cynical as we got older. And of course I had known many of them for years. It's a small city in the end. By virtue of Hong Kong's constricted topography everybody is bound to know everybody, and if I went to the FCC the following night the same faces would almost certainly be there at the bar. But now unfamiliar countenances darted through the mob.

I saw a photographer coming down the steps with his equipment slung over his shoulder and for a moment our eyes met with a mutual recognition that startled me. He passed by me and headed for the gates, and as he slipped away I thought I recalled him: the man in the beanie on the island who had been taking pictures of the lighthouse. I was so sure of it that I followed him out onto Dundas Street and watched him cross that street alone toward Dundas Square. I hesitated, wondering if it was worth abandoning the hospital at that point, and then decided to follow him before it was too late. He was walking quickly, shoulders hunched, and the streets were crowded because of the market on Tung Choi Street.

He had in fact turned into that street, and as I scuttled after him I reached a corner among the market stalls just as he passed a small Thai place I knew called Tom Yum. I had to half run to keep within range of him.

Soon, throwing a glance over one shoulder, his pace relented and he strolled more leisurely under the whirring air-conditioning units set into the facades and the vertical stacks of laundry lines, his camera swinging under his left armpit. He was not lingering for the moment, and if he did linger I had nothing planned to say to him. Soon we were threading our way through the goldfish market, and there, for a minute or so, he paused. Under the lights that illuminated wall after wall of goldfish suspended in plastic bags of water and cages of twittering songbirds, I saw his face a little better. He was a man of about fifty, a little too ostentatiously dressed to be inconspicuous, in black sneakers and an indigo cotton jacket.

He stepped into one of the fish shops with their tanks lit red and purple and examined some of the specimens, gazing up at them as if he was considering a purchase. Then, exiting a little tentatively, he looked both ways and resumed his progress down Tung Choi until he had reached a crossing filled with yet more stores brimming with puppies and baby rabbits and yet more helpless goldfish. There he swung off into the streets of Mong Kok and I followed at a distance of a block.

We fell into the crowds of Argyle Street and it was not long before I was struggling to keep up with him. Step by step he slipped away among the bodies, and I felt that he knew he was being followed and had avoided me skillfully. Yet it had surely not been me who had interested him out on Kau Pei Chau.

Reluctantly, and feeling out of breath, I gave up and stopped by a stall to get an ice cream. Eating it, I retraced my steps back to the hospital, where Cunningham was still loitering by the doors waiting for his break. He looked as if he had been impaled by his own disappointment. Still, he had enough tact not to ask me where I had gone and suggested instead that we give up on the wounded student and go to Spring Deer for Peking duck with two friends of his, a Sri Lankan journalist called Sonny Bawa and an Australian businessman, Dan Moyers, who often gave Cunningham leads and contacts inside the government.

I knew the two gentlemen a little and detested them unequivocally, but at the same time it was a necessary part of the job to sometimes hang out with the detestables in order to keep one's ear to the ground in feverish times. Both of them were assiduous gossipmongers, eavesdroppers, conspiracy enthusiasts, and orchestrators of spy networks: dinner with them often paid off. I could endure them for an hour and Cunningham would buy me dinner.

We set off along Nathan Road, therefore, where the daily disturbances were under way, and as we skirted around it wearing our press badges the air crackled with the sound of glass breaking, though I couldn't see by whom. In passing, Cunningham pointed out that it was the police smashing bottles from a stockpile they had found so that they couldn't be used as missiles. Behind us and farther up the same road the first tear gas round had been fired from another police line and the wind blew it down at our heels. Miniature Stonehenges made of bricks had begun to appear on the roads by then and around them the young black-clads stood with their woks ready to smother the gas canisters, in their scuba masks and ad hoc body armor, not yet tensed by an imminent confrontation. Gas smoke wafted over us, and as we hurried to get away from it I noticed how calm they appeared, almost diffident. I thought of them now as Rebecca's comrades, which only endeared me to them even more. By Chungking

Mansions the air cleared and we went down Mody at a more relaxed pace. Spring Deer, supposedly a haunt of gangsters back in the day, was at the top of a narrow flight of stairs, and at one of its humdrum tables, surrounded by lush floral wallpaper, the physical majesty of the Australian was startlingly paired with the severe thinness of the bespectacled Bawa. Only ideology, the admiration for Mao's state, I thought, could have brought them together so intimately and so ridiculously.

One of the staff in a funereal black waistcoat had already brought over the first bottle of red and the heat of the packed room seemed to draw me back to happier times—of all the lost-to-memory nights I had gotten drunk by myself at Spring Deer among the old-timers.

WE ORDERED THREE PEKING DUCKS because the Australian insisted, and extra bulletins of the heavy, doughy pancakes for which Spring Deer is known. Moyers had also ordered sea cucumbers and steamed ham.

"So you came from the hospital?" Moyers said to Cunningham directly, his eyes narrowing on a target inside the other man's emotions.

"Editor's orders."

"I told Sonny here it wasn't worth going—it served that ankle biter right and everyone knows it. It's time we stopped glorifying protesters with coverage. I know Gyle here will disagree but I've seen the footage. That kid was throwing bricks, for Christ's sake."

"Bricks versus bullets," I said. "A fine contest."

"No, a brick can kill a man. Easy."

Cunningham shook Bawa's hand. "How are you, Sonny? I haven't seen you much on the street."

The Sri Lankan was cool and feline in his way, and a faint smile came to the lips.

"Oh, they're all the same after a while, those events. I got bored of them. I have problematic lungs, too. Enough is enough."

"I hear you. I haven't been out much myself," Cunningham said.

"What about you?" Bawa said to me.

"I've been laying low."

"Myself," Moyers said, continuing his own train of thought, "I think they should bring in the tanks."

Cunningham took off his jacket and slung it over his chair and I saw that his shirt was rotten with accumulated sweat.

"Tanks," he muttered, "always the solution."

Moyers turned to Bawa:

"Cunny here has seen a lot of tanks. But he's better known for his sexual practices with ladies of the night. I say of the night, but in fact he doesn't mind ladies of the day as well."

"He's calling me a musketeer," Cunningham said to me. "But my musketeering days are long over. I sit by the radio now."

"That's where you belong. Gyle, looks like you just got a dose of the old pepper. You want me to pour a bottle over your head?"

"I think that would be unpleasant."

"Is that right? So did you get to see the weasel in his hospital bed?"

"Not even close."

"I thought not. You wasted your time, then."

Bawa said, "All the same. I hope they arrest him when he's patched up."

Moyers was done up in a poplin suit with wide lapels, his stomach bursting forth in a riot of mother-of-pearl buttons. Before the troubles he hadn't been a bad sort, but civil unrest was always bad for business and his accounts had suffered. Like many expats, the indigenous youth irritated him with their tendency to demolish Chinese banks and branches of Starbucks licensed to Maxim's Caterers. The latter were reviled for their sympathies with Beijing. I imagined he hadn't been so vehement a few months earlier but crisis had drawn out the inner man, as it always does. After a few minutes his initial vehemence subsided and I asked him what he had been doing with himself during the days of riot and abandon.

"Me? Nothing different. But Sonny here had an interesting day. Didn't you, Sonny?"

Sonny had not gone to the hospital, it was true, but he had gone to a morgue all the same.

"A morgue?" Cunningham said.

"They found a girl in the harbor this morning. I heard about it from the police."

The number of bodies being fished out of Victoria Harbour was growing, most of them young, most of them women—or so I had heard on the grapevine. Their pictures appeared in the local yellow tabloid press, classified as suicides. Some of them were. But all? The photographers had somehow wormed their way into the confidential freezer compartments of various morgues.

This trade in imagery went on every day. For their part the police said nothing: there were few investigations. And so the grapevine had things to say about it. According to gossips the girls were picked off the streets for rioting, raped, and then disposed of. No one could say if this was true. There was no proof either way. But there were also middle-aged men, hundreds of them, found in waste lots and empty garages and bedsits with torn flesh and mangled legs. "Suicides" that nobody believed were suicides. It was why Bawa, in his curious way, was hunting down bodies in morgues. Not because he wanted to publicize them but because he wanted to explain them away as innocent deaths. His motive for doing so was double-edged: he was on the government's side, as far as his sympathies went, and yet his line of work as a journalist made an association with the police profitable for him. He was friends with them and believed in their honor. I wondered what he thought when he heard crowds of hundreds chanting "rapists"—*sik long*—at the constabulary he admired but who were now dressed more like an occupying army than a police force. Once again the grapevine had proved victorious over the mainstream press. Bawa was one of those men who have an ancestral fear of disorder. Even authoritarian rule by Beijing was better than disorder. If that rule meant throwing a few rioters into the harbor after a bout of perhaps unintentional violence on the part of the police, it was on balance better than the alternative, native democracy, which would mean chaos, litter, and a falling income.

In this perverse, almost patriotic spirit, depending on

one's persuasion, Bawa trawled the morgues. Earlier that day he had received a tip-off from one of his police contacts that another young girl had been spotted in the sea by a passing tugboat and the police had gone out to pick up the body with as much secrecy as they could manage in the circumstances. The press, diverted elsewhere, had missed it and the girl had been brought to shore. Bawa had gone down to the morgue about two hours afterward. The body was partially clothed and she was still wearing a short jacket. The police had seemed agitated about it. At about six, as momentum was gathering around the tale of the shot student inside Kwong Wah Hospital, the officials at the morgue had made calls for relatives to come and identify the body. They must have found some clue to her identity in the jacket pockets. Bawa himself had not been allowed in to see her. He had been obliged to wait outside while an officer quietly filled him in on the details as if the information was understood to be confidential. It was, without question, a suicide, the officer had said, and Bawa repeated it to me with a grimly straight face that revealed not the slightest doubt of the official story. Of course, the police never lied or even exaggerated to their friends in the media, and here Bawa was certainly a friend.

"But as I was waiting at the morgue, writing in my notebook, I noticed a limousine drawing up outside and a man getting out. I thought I recognized him from the gossip rags. I think Jimmy Tang is a friend of yours, isn't he, Adrian?"

I had to dampen down the immediate surprise and pressed my lips together for a moment before speaking.

"Jimmy?"

"I was sure it was him and so was the officer. He might have been lying, of course. But why would he lie to me?"

I looked at Cunningham as if it was I who had been caught out and it must have been comical because Moyers couldn't help a smile. Not knowing what to say, I blurted out something heavily predictable:

"Tang was there?"

"As I said," Bawa went on calmly, with an effect of ice in his voice. "He came in and greeted the officers and seemed so wrapped up in the situation that he didn't see me."

"Do you know him?" Moyers asked.

"We were at university together. I've known him for over a quarter of a century."

Bawa nodded, indicating that he knew this already.

"Then maybe you know why he came down there," he said. "I certainly don't know. Do you think it's possible that he might have known the dead girl?"

"That's preposterous. Why would he?"

"I can't say. He was there and they let him in. He seemed pretty tense." He paused. "I don't want to write a story about it, if that's what you're thinking. Not at all. But it's pretty interesting, don't you think?"

My first instinct was to protect Jimmy, so all I said was that it couldn't have been him.

"But I'm sure it was."

My mind was racing ahead. How many women did Jimmy have in his orbit? Lovers, acolytes, favor-seekers, distant or proximate admirers, friends of the family. But Bawa then said that there had been no great scene of grief. Jimmy had spent a minute inside the room and then exited calmly enough. His innate reserve must have come in useful if she had truly been an intimate of his.

I said, "It's odd more than anything. Did you find out the girl's name?"

"They wouldn't say. I don't think she was some poor local student. The fact that the Tangs were involved—"

But not necessarily in the plural, I wanted to say.

"Isn't that the Jimmy Tang who races yachts?" Moyers put in casually, although he knew exactly who it was and how many yachts he had raced. "Don't they call him Terrible Tang? And he came down to the morgue?"

I said I really had no idea. *Terrible Tang*. It was a name I'd heard applied to him, created in order to evoke his notorious womanizing. *Terrible Tang turns up to identify the body of a young woman*—the soap opera wrote itself. But it could have been any number of girls because now that I thought about it more carefully I had met only a handful of them. I filed through them mentally now, but rejecting at once the idea that it might be Rebecca. I had been with her the previous night and there had been no sign that anything was amiss. And surely there is always a sign. As for the others, I had seen a few of them at parties over the previous three or four years, invariably young and avid for advancement in the city's suffocating social hierarchy. Now that I thought about them more carefully, scenes from the past resurfaced while I held my tongue. A face that flashed out of the dark one night at Pierre as Jimmy and his consort-of-the-night waved good night across a packed room in paper party hats; a gallery

opening somewhere in Central on a hot summer night, a
woman introduced briefly by a name I couldn't now recall,
her face covered in glitter, seen again by chance a week later
at a charity function at Belon, even more striking under the
globe-shaped lamps.

But who had she been? I didn't follow Jimmy's liaisons as
if they were breaking news and I rarely asked him about his
private life. Bawa, however, didn't know this and it was clear
that he was expecting a juicy tip from me, even one tossed
out unknowingly by the unconscious.

But I said, watching my every word, "I'm afraid I can't
give you a suggestion as to who the girl might be. Maybe it's
a high-society thing."

By this I meant that people in that elevated and, to Bawa,
enigmatic world had their own rules and made their own discreet arrangements with the authorities.

He said, "Yes, it's a high-society thing, all right. That
much is obvious. But you know that world much better than
I do."

"Tang's been up to no good," Moyers sighed as the Peking ducks arrived, borne out on castored carts by the ancient waiters. "That's for sure."

The showmanship carving was upon us. The opening of
the bamboo baskets of steaming pancakes and the distribu-
tion of spring onions. Within a few seconds his remark had
been left to one side and I was grateful not to have to make
anything more of it. I could also sense a gloating desire to
provoke me into saying something rash, which would be remembered for a long time and without benevolence.

For among us there was always a nagging tension about larger things. I was seen to be pro-Western in my sympathies, whereas they had a much greater respect for China than, say, for the United States. It was a matter of temperament. They believed in China as a superior *idea* whose time had come.

They never told me what this idea really was, beyond a sentimental and intimidating idea of China herself: the beautiful suspension bridges, the majestic airports, the 65 million empty apartments, the electric taxis, the steel-production statistics, the salvation from absolute poverty of 300 million souls none of whom our intrepid journalists had ever met. You would have heard the same arguments for Germany at dinner parties in Surrey in 1938. The autobahns, the production figures, the workers' holidays and free child care, the nationalized health care and the low crime rates: a nation speeding ahead of us on gleaming rails. I remembered reading about D. H. Lawrence walking through a German city in the late 1920s and tasting the strange electricity in the air, a palpable change of ions. But such an observation would never convince anyone of anything. And so against the Bawas and the Moyerses and their belief in China's supremacy there was no counterargument I could make that they would ever accept. If you mentioned a mendacious Chinese trade practice of any kind they would cry "Confessions of an Economic Hitman!" If you mentioned Xinjiang's camps they would smirk, wave a hand, and talk about Wounded Knee. The endless false equivalences, the shifting sands, the curious and obstinate state of self-enchanting.

To an observer that was exactly how I had come to think of it: a form of enchantment. But we are all prey to enigmatic enchantment in one form or another. I was, therefore, reluctant to moralize too severely. It all depends on what you want to be enchanted by or what you want to be disenchanted with. The kind of people who were in love with the idea of a rising China tended to be the kinds who relished the idea of a declining America and who consequently loved to pronounce upon the latter's problems. China's problems they tended not to know so much about. What you don't know can still enchant you.

However, I still wanted to know from Bawa what the girl in the morgue had died from. If it was suicide, had she drowned herself in the harbor as the police were claiming?

"Let's leave aside the conspiracy theories, shall we?" Moyers put in suddenly, as if to sweep this conversation away and put it in the trash where it belonged. "All this lugubrious gossip about bodies in the harbor. I remember them ten years ago and they can't all have been murdered by the state. Jesus. I'd worry about the Americans more than dead girls in Victoria Harbour if I were you. Some things are real."

"It's not a binary choice," Cunningham retorted, but avoiding Moyers's eye because it wasn't worth a full-blown row.

"At least you could tell me which morgue it was," I said. "Every person dead on-site goes to the public mortuary. Was it Victoria?" It was, Bawa said. I knew that shabby bend in the road where the Victoria Public Mortuary stood near the pier in Kennedy Town, right above the water and circled by gulls. I had passed within its dirty white walls on two occasions, covering society suicides myself, and recalled its air of distance from the city's life, like the abattoirs no one wants to see, not even in passing. That was where all the alleged suicides went, all the unknown deaths. The Sai See refuse collection center was next to it, an unfortunate symbol for those inclined to notice, and it was hard to imagine Jimmy rolling out of his limousine in such a setting.

"I don't suppose," I ventured, "that they would consider letting me go down there?"

"Not a chance, *gwailo*. Even if you knew the girl they'd never let you in there."

Only then did I begin to feel a chill descend from the dark cobwebs of the dining room and touch my upper back.

"In fact," Bawa countered, "I was going to ask *you* a favor. I was wondering if you could talk to the esteemed Mr. Tang yourself about this? You know, just as a friend. Just to see how he reacts. Any information you can get out of him will help identify this girl. It won't be easy but I think you could find out."

He leaned forward a little, momentarily agitated by all the little facts he wasn't going to tell me just yet.

"They're going to cover this one up. I mean, the Tangs are going to cover it up—that I can guarantee."

"But what about the police?"

"They will want to do the same. It's always how they deal with society suicides."

"So you think it's a society girl?"

A calm smile had spread across his face and he tapped the table with an emphatic little finger, on which he wore a gold ring that gave his whole person an appealing vulgarity. I noticed as if for the first time his cheap sand-colored suit and light rose shirt with a garish diamond motif pattern. I didn't like him, or his taste in clothes. The antagonism among him, Moyers, and myself had a whiff of old-time colonial resentment. We all came from Commonwealth nations and we all had our suspicions about one another. For them, it was the future that would offer revenge. They weren't exactly *wumao,* regime trolls, but they weren't far off. The dead girl in the Victoria mortuary was just a bargaining chip to get something on Jimmy. A scandal he could use in one of his columns, a tip to the secret police, a lever he could use to lift off the ground a power greater than himself. It wasn't clear what he wanted. But every hack wants something, always casting his line to catch a fish of one kind or another. And it was true that now I wanted to know who the girl in the morgue was and why Jimmy had gone down there to identify her. I did indeed want to talk to him and find out what had happened. Even as his friend I wasn't entitled to know, but I felt offense at the idea that I might be denied it from his own lips. At the same time I felt confident that he would tell me the truth—in his own elliptical way, of course. He would tell me long before Bawa ever found out. With that, in any case, dinner concluded and inevitably I paid, even though I was probably no more in the money than any of them. Noblesse oblige.

ONCE WE WERE BACK on the island side I decided on the spur of the moment to ignore the Sri Lankan's advice and diverted the taxi to Kennedy Town. It was a long ride out west to the quieter shore just beyond the last of the tower blocks, whose lights were going off one by one as we passed below them, past the faded white walls of the Jockey Club Clinic and the little park in Sai Ning Street. Opposite it lay the modest mortuary, but I asked the driver to drop me off instead inside the bus station next door, which was part of the China Merchants Wharf development.

I asked him to wait for me there for a good tip, and walked slowly back to the mortuary on the same road. At the door were two *po-po,* or police, who I knew were not usually stationed there. When I appeared, a snooping foreigner and therefore an unwelcome vision, they tensed visibly and made a fuss about my ID. My ID would not have made much difference, however. Seeing that I had a press badge they categorically refused to let me enter the premises. A far-flung question in English was not going to be answered but I spoke to them in Putonghua and one of them spoke it fluently. I was still a little buzzed from the bad wine and I felt my insolence rising. I persisted in throwing a few awkward questions at them right there on the steps, saying that I knew a girl had arrived at the mortuary some time before and that I had an interest in seeing her. The two men called in a senior officer, who pushed open the glass doors and barked at me to step back down onto the street. He, too, demanded to see my ID and it was then that I realized I had perhaps made a small mistake: my name would now be remembered. Who was I, he wanted to know, and what was it to me? To which I couldn't make much of a reply.

"Then fuck off," he shouted in English, waving a fist like a mace on a medieval battlefield.

I walked back to the wharf building and went through the unmanned gate onto the jetty, thinking that I had indeed made an error but not an immense one. Yet I was uneasy, uncertain. The sea was calm under moonlight and as ever the scattered islands shone in their haze. I sat on the wharf and wore down a Hint of Mint cigarette, thinking over the mannerisms of the three policemen whose duty was to prevent entry to a public facility with such bad language. The way they had reacted made Bawa's tale about Jimmy more likely than not, though there was hardly any proof one way or the other. As the Chinese say, he was certainly *ẓau san ngai*, in the shit, but literally "crawling from head to toe with ants." Beyond that I couldn't say what he had done or how he was involved. Men with money move in ways very different from the ways available to someone like myself. In the great coral reef of the city they moved like octopuses, knowing caves and niches that I could only guess at. Nevertheless, you always assume that you can ask a friend anything if it's important enough.

FOR SEVERAL DAYS, with that in mind, I called Jimmy at regular intervals only to find that his voicemail was perpetually activated and was being used to screen his whereabouts. It seemed to corroborate Bawa's insinuations. As for Rebecca, she had never given me her number, and there was no way of reaching her. Jimmy himself seemed to have gone to ground up in the Mid-Levels, sequestered by his family perhaps. It was not like him, and it was unusual for him not to return a call. And yet three days later I got word of a party that he had thrown on the night after my dinner at Spring Deer. It was said that Hong Kong's richest man, the superbly named Li Ka-Shing, had been there, as well as Jimmy's formidable father-in-law, Rodney Chow. Once again, it was only gossip and I had a feeling that it was not even true. It might even have been disinformation emanating from Bawa himself to needle me. Nevertheless, it made me want to go looking for Jimmy's innumerable friends and associates to see if they would let slip a hint or two. In the event, they had apparently been sworn to omertà. Nor did I find any mention of Rebecca herself. Around them, out of nowhere, an almost complete silence had descended. It was as if, for a brief and glamorous period, they had monopolized the dance floor and then walked off without anyone but myself noticing. I thought that perhaps it was due to an agreement between themselves. I could well understand the societal pressures they were both continually under. But then I wondered just how fully I understood the tight-knit warp and weave of a society like Hong Kong: incestuous, gossipy, given to rumors and backstabbing, its money all wrapped up in a few clans, always ready to flee to foreign parts if the going got rough. Insecurity and a nervous fight-or-flight mentality plague the collective subconscious of the wealthy classes. "How long have we got?" they seem to be perpetually asking themselves in their nightmares. "How long will our happiness last?" There were no answers to either ques-

tion and so they tried hard to maintain their outward respectability. Jimmy was never as free as he pretended to be. And
shortly after my visit to the morgue, indeed only a day later,
that same society discovered why Jimmy had gone to ground
in the first place. The headlines were typically incriminating,
and I quickly came across one that summed them all up: "Society Darling Known as Terrible Tang Seen on Yacht with
Beautiful 'friend.' An Affair?" Photographs began to appear
everywhere of Jimmy and Rebecca together.

The story was broken by the tabloid *Apple Daily*, which
was owned by the anti-government garment industry mag-
nate Jimmy Lai. Did we not all remember why Lai had
named his paper thus? If Adam and Eve, he is said to have
stated, did not eat of the forbidden apple, would there be any
evil and therefore any news? On its news site, the gossip
about Jimmy Tang lit up the city. Even among the usual buf-
fet of celebrity scandals, gangster tales, gambling news,
semi-fabrications about sensational suicides, grisly traffic accidents, and financial crimes it flared like a garish comet
across the city's consciousness.

But there was something else. I instantly recognized the
setting of the images. It was the island where we had moored
together on Jimmy's yacht. And in some of those shots I
could also see myself, the obscure unnamed hack whom only
a few people would recognize or comment upon, one of
whom might certainly include Jimmy's wife, Melissa. It
meant that in her eyes I was now fingered as an accomplice to
a bit of lighthearted adultery, just as she had expected of me
only a few weeks before.

That, then, was one family whose threshold I could no longer cross. It was a disappointment, admittedly, but at the same time it provided a simple explanation for Jimmy's disappearance. He had been caught in the midst of an indiscretion and there was no more to it than that. For a while, the realization calmed me. It was a mere flap over an affair. He was embarrassed, that was all. Rebecca, too, I imagined. Two displeased families. It wasn't the end of the world, and people in their society would snigger for a week or two and then forget about it. Such things came and went all the time.

I let Jimmy and Rebecca disappear as they wished and returned to my own life, which had become more ungrounded as the days went by. It was as if my employer was quite happy to put me out to pasture for a while, regardless of what he had said to my face. A week went by, then, and as I had expected the scandal faded a little, eclipsed by others. Scandals, after all, are ten a penny in this city; they come in a constant flow. The most recent one instantly effaces the one preceding it. Yet Jimmy's momentary disgrace didn't vanish altogether. People talk, as if their tongues have a life of their own. I heard whispers of it around me sometimes at the journalists' bars, at the FCC among the scribes of the night, at the Old Man, where I had returned in spite of my anxiety about the place. *Terrible Tang and his fling*. It was remarkable that no one had yet asked me why I had been on the yacht that day. I assumed at first that they didn't want to say anything to my face even if they had known it was me, but it was equally possible that I simply never crossed anyone's mind even when evidence for my existence in a compromising photograph was not difficult to discern. A ghost in other people's machines. They had seen me and I had not registered as any-one whose identity was worth investigating. In its way it let me off the hook. Yet Jimmy never called me back. He had gone to ground and even for him I was now nonexistent. I had slipped, in his mind, into a different dimension.

SEVEN

YOU HAVE TO ADMIRE A CITY WHOSE RICHEST MAN IS called Ka-Shing. As soon as I heard his name, I remembered that at the beginning of the current protests he had come out publicly with a statement that quoted a poem by the Tang writer Li Xian. *The melon of Huangtai*, Ka-Shing had written with maximum cryptic intent, *cannot bear to be picked again*.

After creating an uproar on Weibo, the statement was banned in China because it was understood to mean: something that has been attacked cannot be attacked a second time without losing all its value. Did that mean Hong Kong itself? Ka-Shing's spokesmen answered that he was evoking the Lotus Sutra, a doctrine with which Communists are not entirely comfortable. The Lotus Sutra is a series of slightly fantastical dramas and parables considered by many in both China and Japan as the final and most important revelation of the teaching of Buddha. A bodhisattva called Wonderful Sound visits Buddha from a distant planet, stupas encrusted with jewels float in the air like spaceships, and Buddha himself saves billions of souls over the course of millennia. Naturally, meanwhile, I know the poem by Li Xian. He, the crown prince, was forced to commit suicide by his mother, Empress

Wu Zetian, in 684. Before killing himself he wrote "The Melon of Huangtai" as a complaint against persecution by the state:

> *Growing melons beneath Huangtai*
> *Hanging heavily, many grow ripe,*
> *Pick one, the others will be fine*
> *Pick two, fewer are left on the vine . . .*
> *And if there is any more reaping*
> *You will end up with an empty vine.*

It was easy to imagine Li Ka-Shing and Jimmy quoting it together over a cigar on his balcony. Did they really know each other? Either way I thought a lot about Ka-Shing and the melons in the days and weeks after the publication of the incriminating photographs, which soon spread from *Apple Daily* to all the other tabloids. One had to give credit to the courage even of his veiled references to the adamant authority all around us. I kept thinking that if Ka-Shing could say such things, implying without too much concealment the view that tyrants always eventually undo themselves by repressing too many of their subjects, why couldn't I, when I had a British passport in my back pocket? But then, when I thought about what had become of the Western press itself, the irony disappeared. Journalists in our own countries were being silenced and curtailed on a daily basis. To the great satisfaction of our rulers, to the owners of our communicative platforms, we were becoming more like China with every day that passed.

After a week, in any case, the phone rang one morning

and the voice at the other end of it surprised me. There Jimmy was at last, resurrected from the dead. Chipper and innocent, apologetic and cajoling, pleading work and family as the chronically evasive always do. In the event I found that I didn't mind his silence. I was pretty sure that my inquiries to his friends had gotten back to him. He must have heard all my messages as well and turned them over in his mind. In those messages I had mentioned the photographs and that I wanted to ask him what he was going to do about them.

"I'm sorry about the radio silence, comrade," he declared, breezily. "Now, what are you doing today? Shall we go to Chan and get suits? It's my treat."

I laughed. "A suit is your idea of a treat?"

"I thought it might be a fun way to say sorry for being so rude. Besides, my father-in-law has been pouring money over my head. I think they're trying to keep me quiet."

"It's a pretty strange thing to offer, Jimmy."

"Is it? I don't see why. We can talk about the serious stuff afterward. I'll take you to Mott 32 for lunch."

"I'd like that more than the suit."

"It'll probably cost more. Then we can talk about the press."

Ah, I thought, so you do need me after all.

"I heard from someone that you had dinner with Li Ka-Shing," I said, more irritably than I intended.

"Where did you hear that? I don't even know the man. Do you?"

"Of course I don't."

"Then how could you know such a thing?"

"Some idiotic journalist mentioned it to me."

"Naturally. And you didn't laugh at him?"

"I didn't know what to think."

"Well, now you do."

I left it at that, and then I said that sure, I would meet him at Chan if he wished.

"But you really don't need to buy me a suit, Jimmy."

"Come off it. It's nothing to me. We're comrades, aren't we? The least I can do is to get you to retire one of your shitty suits."

Later that day I walked up the steps of the Entertainment Building in Central and got coffee at the little shop at the foot of the gloomy elevators. Queens Road Central outside had sunk into apathy as the pedestrians melted away in the sunshine leaving a hundred cars caught in a malevolent spell. The engines ticked over as some obstruction out of view prevented them from moving. The elevators were as ghostly as the street outside. W. W. Chan's premises lay at the end of a chilly corridor, a simple glass door and a display case with a single suit modeled inside it. But within the gentlemen's-club-style room with its padded armchairs Jimmy was already present in a sharkskin suit talking with his cutter. We were the only ones there since business had worsened, and Jimmy turned on the charm to make me feel less awkward.

"You know Adrian Gyle, don't you?" he said to the tailor. "He's one of the world's most famous journalists. Or so he says. I believe you made him a morning coat once."

"Yes, we did. I remember Mr. Gyle very well."

We shook hands and Jimmy told me that he had picked out a fabric for me. It was a mid-gray Loro Piana Prince of Wales Super 130 and he added that he really would buy me the suit. While I was being measured in the mirror room, which lies behind the main sales room, he called ahead to Mott 32 in the Standard Chartered Bank Building and procured a lunch table for us. I came back out into the room and we chose Bemberg linings and horn buttons for our coats and mulled the question of monograms and cigar pockets. The mood between us was relaxed. His body language did not seem in any way abnormal. We discussed the barchetta breast pocket issue, patch pockets or flapped, lapel depth and angle, notched or peak, single- or double-breasted, pleats or not, cuffs or not, high or medium rise in the trousers, side adjusters over belts, and the break of the trousers. It took half an hour and Jimmy drew it out as long as he could. He had noticed, he said quietly to me alone when the others were busy elsewhere, that Chan had turned in recent years to a softer, more Neapolitan cut and away from the former house style rooted in British norms. They were doing fewer roped shoulders and more *spalla camicia* sleeveheads with a delicate puckering and a less-structured silhouette. It was what younger men wanted and so it had become what some older men wanted as well. He prattled on about it with his casual expertise: how much he loved Caccioppoli fabrics from Naples with their summery patterns and subtle colors, how much he loved the mohairs from Standeven, especially their monochrome puppytooth and their formal Blackstorm range, and how recently he had been converted by the wise men of W. W. Chan to the glories of tweed and W. W. Bill linen.

"A tobacco suit is all the rage," he said as we were reaching the elevators again and the staff from Chan had held open the doors for us. "I should have gotten you a Bill tobacco number. Very useful in our unsartorial climate. Next time. There will be a next time, Adrian—I hope you know that, don't you?"

"I'll never wear these suits, as I'm sure you know."

"Yes, but they'll be hanging like ghosts in your closet, filling you with guilt. You'll feel ashamed when you put on your normal junk. And you can wear them to my parties."

"Your wife would notice at once."

He made a face, his arms swinging, entirely unconcerned by anything as far as I could tell.

"That she would, comrade. But you'd just tell her you got a windfall from a dead uncle. We all have windfall uncles. Even broke bastards like you."

"You mean she would bawl you out over three thousand dollars?"

"*She* wouldn't—she'd get her mother to bawl me out."

We stepped out onto the street only to find that it had been transformed by the arrival of clouds which had in turn blotted out the sun. The whole mood had changed. A dash of typhoon rain was coming in on a hot wind. Nevertheless, as we walked to Mott 32, our bodies tensed against the rising wind. The great, oddball buildings had become somber and satanic as the edge of the typhoon touched them. At the Standard Chartered we went up the steep flight of steps hounded by the first drops of rain. The long escalator ride down to the restaurant in the basement returned us to sheltered security. To my surprise the place was bustling. Escapism in times of crisis: restaurants do well. The flower arrangements, the splashes of calligraphy on the walls, the industrial ceilings, and the dim dark-gold lighting were instantly refreshing. Thankfully I forgot the heavy atmosphere at W. W. Chan, getting measured for a suit I didn't even want. Now instead was the hour of dim sum, of *lo bak gao* and black truffle *xiao long bao* and pu'er tea. The glutton in me leaped to attention. This far deep into the earth we wouldn't hear a thing even if the storm hit Standard Chartered directly. It was a bunker for those who could pay. Jimmy was feeling talkative, too, and that helped me forget the previous few hours. I devoured the radish cakes rolled in oily chili sauce and listened to him describe how his father-in-law had given him a stern lecture about falling into line with what he called the new regime in town: the Communist Party. It was ironic that since the protests had begun many members of their sprawling family were buying houses in London and Vancouver, seeking out British or American passports and spiriting their capital away into empty condos in Bangkok. Your left hand need not acknowledge what your right hand is doing behind your own back. But all the same, the family had to show a united front.

"That bunch of grifters. Psychopaths, playboys, tightwads, and parasites. You can't imagine how terrified they are. And *I* am the one who is embarrassing *them*? They are either running for the hills or bowing down to the new rulers. What is it the Gauls said to the Romans? You make a desert and call it peace."

"Tacitus."

"Yeah, Tacitus—exactly." His eyes lit up and he smiled with delight. "Julius Caesar. So Xi is our Julius Caesar and my family are the Gauls who submit. Brilliant."

Pleased with this scholarly memory, he beamed at me with a dumpling suspended between his chopsticks, where it disintegrated in slow motion.

"There's a scramble for the exit," he went on, "and soon we're all going to be living like rats in California. Like *rats*. Everyone in California lives like a rat. Well, not everyone. But me—I will certainly be living like a rat over there. An escaped rat. A rat of the *ancien régime*."

"And Melissa is all right with exile in California?" I said, not sure how serious he was being.

"God no, of course she's not OK with it. She has no reason to leave. She swears she'll stay here. She doesn't mind the Chinese system one bit. She admires it. It seems we are headed for a bust-up."

"You could stay, too."

"Could is not *would*."

"All the same, you could."

"But I'm not going to live under those cretins. On the bended knee and all that. Not a chance."

On the bended knee with a fat silver spoon rammed down one's throat: it wasn't the end of the world. More than that, it was in many ways attractive. What will people endure simply to obtain a bit of security and stability? Almost anything. It depends what their greatest fears are. But in any case the bended knee was hardly a uniquely Chinese phenomenon. Who did not bend the knee in the West? With a bit more fuss and noise, but ultimately bending the knee to capitalism in exchange for health, safety, and a long life. In fact, millions *dreamed* of having a silver spoon rammed down their throat while bending the knee. It was their Utopia! Jimmy got worked up, managing to snarl as he talked, like a Punch puppet.

"I don't have to tell you that my father-in-law, and my father, too, for that matter, went all lunatic on me about those pictures in the *Apple Daily*. And everywhere else, alas. They knew exactly how to get at me. It was a blow aimed with real precision, I'll give them that. Can you imagine what Chow had to say to me? It was a ritual humiliation. He called me into his office and gave me a dressing down for an hour. He threw a glass of whisky in my face and I had to stand there and take it. Nothing I could do. He called me a punk. That was the actual word he used. Coming from a punk supreme, that was a bit rich, but I had to take it. How do you think that felt?"

"I think you'll live."

"Don't get clever on me, Gyle. He threatened cutting off the money as well. You know how it is. Dishonored his daughter and all that. Well, he has a point, I suppose." He slumped back in his chair.

"But you have your own money, don't you?"

"Yes, but not—how can I put it?"

"—on the same scale?"

"Thank you. It's not a small thing to be sniffed at. It's hundreds of millions. I have shares. It's complicated. In any case, then he calmed down a bit."

"Did he ask you who took the pictures?"

"Of course he did. But how do I know? He even suggested that it was you—that you set it up. Can you imagine?"

There was a moment of dull astonishment inside my mind

that I tried to keep under control, yet I was unable to stop my mouth opening. I saw at once that it gave Jimmy a quiet pleasure. "Don't worry, I talked him out of that one. But he asked me about you and I had to tell him. Even though you've already met him at my parties, he doesn't remember anyone who isn't important. I told him adamantly that it had nothing to do with you. That said, I do have to ask if you think that anyone you know might have gotten the idea into his head—even if it's someone you know only slightly—"

I said it was so ridiculous I wouldn't even entertain the idea.

"I thought so, too. But he was right about one thing, namely that there is a possibility of blackmail, isn't there?"

I said, "A blackmailer would have shot his bolt by now, I would have thought. The pictures are already out there."

"But he might know more. How do I know what other pictures he might have held back? Think about it." His voice had lowered. "How do we know? We don't know anything about him."

"Paparazzi."

He leaned back a little and a terrible smile got the better of him.

"Spoken like one! But none of us really know. My father-in-law thinks it's something else."

"Such as?"

"I don't know. Political associations—I mean, the associations of the girl I've been with the last few weeks."

"You're not an enemy of the state, Jimmy. None of us are."

"But she is," he sighed. "She very much is."

It was enough for them to keep an eye on him, to bring him under control with a bit of subtle blackmail, if that was what it was. Did I not see? That was always how they worked. The smear, the discrediting of a reputation. It was a warning shot across his bows.

"How has Melissa been taking it?"

Shiftily, he glanced down at his nails as he always did when he felt that he was in a tightening spot.

"Oh, it was a scene straight out of *Gone With the Wind*. Barns burning and all that. I just had to bear it and apologize and grovel. It was ghastly."

"Did she forgive you eventually?"

"She degenerated into a frigid calm."

"It must have been a shock. Don't tell me you were surprised?"

"Surprised, no. Furious, yes."

"With yourself?"

"No. With that goddamned photographer! I was thinking, Adrian—I am sure you could find him if you looked hard enough. I mean, not just as a favor to me but as a favor to yourself. I'm surprised you haven't taken some flak for it already."

"What do you mean?"

"Your editor hasn't mentioned it to you at all?"

I shook my head as slowly as I could while wondering about that myself. It was a good point; Strick had not mentioned it thus far. For that matter Strick had been uncommonly silent with me of late, more silent than he had ever been in the past.

I said, "As for the photographer, I suppose I could ask around. Someone might have heard something."

Then I wondered if I should tell him about the man I had seen that day and indeed afterward at the hospital. I knew it would set Jimmy off on a paranoid toot but at least I would be coming clean with him about what I knew. There would be a figure—a villain—he could fixate on. In the end, without much compunction, I told him that I had seen the man from the island outside the hospital where I was investigating the shot boy, and that I had chased him through the streets around the hospital. Jimmy fixed me with wide-open eyes as I recounted the pursuit among the birdcages on Tung Choi. He was gripped. I related how I had followed the man until I had lost him among the crowds but that he had certainly been taking pictures at the hospital. It could be deduced, therefore, that he was part of the press corps in some way. But couldn't I track him down by his face?

"Among hundreds of journalists?"

"You'll see him again somewhere."

"Perhaps yes, but who knows when."

His face tensed and, as I had seen once or twice before, a vein or nerve within it seemed to bulge close to his right ear. He wanted to curse aloud but we were seated next to two hawkish old ladies whom he was convinced would recognize him from the papers.

"You know what this means," he went on, his voice lowered, his cheeks reddening. "Not only do I have a family crisis but now I have the threat of blackmail potentially hanging over me."

"Don't tell me you have other women?"

"Not really. But either way that person is obviously stalking me. Don't you think? How did he know to be on the island? You have to admit it's a pretty towering coincidence. In fact, Adrian, I've been wondering something else. I know it sounds paranoid on my part, but what if Rebecca is in on it? It would explain a lot. I know it's far-fetched, but what if?"

"To what end?"

He seemed flustered and a light sweat crystallized on his forehead.

"Oh, I don't know. It's a stab in the dark. But what if she wanted to get back at me. You know?"

I could see where he was coming from. Take down a high-society figure who is sleeping with a protest leader and make a political point by exposing his hypocrisy. Surprisingly, it was not nearly as illogical as I had first assumed. Yet that did not make it probable.

"Get back at you for what?" I asked, innocently.

"I didn't tell you, but she and I had a . . . well, I broke it off. I had to. It was before all this, obviously. But I could see it coming. There was no way we could keep it secret. She took it badly—worse than I thought she would. I didn't think she would take it hard at all, to be honest. Think how young she is. Why would she take it hard? It's *me* who should be taking it hard. And I am. But she made a scene."

"Where?"

"It's too stupid. At Soho House."

"You could at least have picked a tactful spot."

Jimmy grimaced.

"And when was this?"

I wanted to calculate at what point she had been verifiably alive, but Jimmy was deliberately vague, as if he didn't want to say. All he admitted was that they had gone to Soho House for dinner and he hadn't planned to do it then. But the pressure had gotten too much for him, he said. They were in the restaurant area. A lot of people noticed. "It was a royal fuckup," he admitted.

I said, "But they wouldn't have known who you were necessarily."

"I'm sure some did. You never know in this town. The waiters came over and asked us if everything was all right. That's never happened to me before." He was seething, reliving it all again.

"I don't believe a word of it."

"You know," he went on, as if what I said couldn't possibly matter, "you spend all this time with a woman and you think you know who she is and *what* she is and why she is with you. But in the end you know nothing. Absolutely nothing."

He had looked into her eyes at that moment, he said, and saw nothing recognizable at all. Just a hostile emptiness. Naturally he understood it was the shock of an unpleasant moment. He could hardly have expected the scene to go entirely to plan. She had launched into recriminations, accusations, and the violence of the reaction had blindsided him. She told him that he was only doing it because he was afraid of his wife's family. Which was true. But they were unwelcome observations nonetheless. She hadn't tried at all to see it from his point of view, Jimmy said pathetically. Yet he had re-mained quiet, and had tried to calm her down. She wouldn't have it, though.

"That's an unfortunate scene for Soho House," I said.

"It was a farce."

Something in his eye seemed to brighten for a moment.

"So afterward, when the pictures surfaced, I admit I did think it might be her. She might have planned it long before our breakup. But maybe it was for another reason altogether, I don't know. I have to admit to you, if I'm being frank, that I think she's capable of it. She could well have been filled with rage at me. I wouldn't blame her, even."

I didn't buy it, but Jimmy seemed utterly convinced. He said that when they spent the night together she never slept. Messages kept lighting her phone up all night. He had a hunch that it was her fellow conspirators down in the streets. Maybe they wanted something from her, maybe she was even sleeping with him for an ulterior reason, as he had just suggested to me. Then, along these lines, something more had occurred to him. She was there with him purely to get money out of him for the cause, or to cause a scandal that would make him amenable to them. Was it possible? he asked me directly, and I replied that I had no idea. In fact, as far as I was concerned it was not true. His feverish ramblings about this theory felt put-on, as if he were carefully deflecting and leading me astray. And so, little by little, we began to enter new territory in our friendship. I could feel that it was a small game to Jimmy, and that he was sounding out my reactions by testing me and not divulging to me what he really thought. He was lying, in other words, in order to play this game, and his confession was therefore a pseudo-confession. I objected to his insinuation about Rebecca, in any case, and I could see from his reaction that he was not at all surprised or inclined to push back.

"I agree," he conceded mildly. "But it's not impossible either. That's what Melissa and her father said to me. That it was a plot to harm me, to harm them. She was using me all along."

"It's ridiculous."

"All right—"

"Then where is Rebecca now?" He threw up his hands with a touch of melodrama.

"That's what I want to know. If only I *did* know. I didn't see her after that night at Soho House and we stopped communicating. It was necessary. You can understand that."

"Naturally. So that night," I said, "was really the last time you saw her?"

"Absolutely." Didn't I just say so? his tone implied.

So their breakup must have been before I had met her at the China Club. Yet she had mentioned nothing about it to me. Either he was lying now or she had not wanted to bring it up at the time. Come to think of it, she had been quite cool when talking about Jimmy. Perhaps I had missed the clue.

He was still talking, interrupting my train of thought. One night, he said, when he and Melissa had been dining in the main room, the landline phone had rung and Melissa had gotten there before him. He had heard her from the dining room, repeatedly asking "Hello? Hello?" until she had given up and returned to the table. He had then asked her who it had been. She had shrugged, saying only that it must have been a prank call or a wrong number. Yet Melissa had appeared rattled and her mood had changed. It then occurred to him that someone on the other end of the line had maybe spoken to her after all. He watched her face for signs that this might have been the case. She had grown cold and nervous. "It seems odd that people are playing pranks," he had said. As she looked away he had felt certain that someone had indeed spoken to her and she did not want to reveal it.

"I kept thinking all night that the caller had exposed my affair to Melissa and that she was keeping it to herself. But there was no way to prove it."

It was possible, I supposed, that Rebecca had been feeling vengeful and prone to reckless behavior. It would not be in keeping with the individual I thought I knew, but when it came down to it, how well did I know either of them?

"You should call her," I said.

But suddenly, for the first time, I had the feeling that there was no one to call. Rebecca had gone, but I didn't know where. I can't say why I suspected it either. A slow buildup of unease arose within me, and I thought of Bawa then. He had not lied at all—Jimmy had been at the morgue.

"No," he said smoothly, "that would be a terrible idea. I'm sure she hates me now. Either way, I'm not calling her. For all I know, she's gone abroad."

"Abroad?"

He made a small gesture of resignation and caught the eye of a waiter.

"Shall we have another bottle? Come on."

We sailed on, bound to get more incoherent. It was a relief in a way. The skin along my back grew moist, my temples flushed with blood. The wound on my cheek, which by now felt like some sort of old battle scar, grew feverishly hot as well and I feared it would suppurate visibly.

I excused myself and went to the bathrooms, which at Mott 32 are buried inside a small dark-walled labyrinth. I found them empty. Dampening a paper tissue, I tended to the wound, which had indeed flared up, as if it were psychologically connected to my moods. An irrational fear gripped me. All that is solid, as Marx said, melts into air. Not only that, it does so from one moment to the next. Between leaving the table and staring into my own image everything that I thought I knew about Jimmy and his city evaporated. Around me now was empty space, noise, and madness. I gripped the edge of the basin and watched as perspiration rolled down my cheek into the fabric of my collar. Yet the bathroom was cold, as cold as I was. I thought back to his account of the mysterious phone call to his house. Had it been after Bawa had seen him at the morgue, or before? I hadn't asked him the date. Confused, I calmed myself and went back to the table, where Jimmy carried on as if he had noticed nothing unusual about me.

"A toast!" he cried, raising his glass. "Who's better than us?"

It was an old toast from college and I echoed it. Pretty much everyone in this room, I thought to myself, bitterly.

"So what are you going to do now?" I asked, taking a sip of wine and relaxing into my seat.

"I'll stay home and have dinner with Melissa and endure it until she forgives me. It's rather a classic move, but no more parties for me. I'm going to keep my face out of those magazines for a bit. Maybe I'll grow up, as her family keep asking me to do."

"And about Rebecca, you really don't know where she is?"

"You'll have to take my word for it. Maybe you can find her yourself. Why the sudden interest, Adrian?"

His eyes sharpened and I was forced to take a quick step back.

"To be honest, I'm just worried about her."

He took this in his stride, revealing nothing. It was not the moment to confront him with my suspicions and I could hardly throw Bawa's testimony in his face.

He said, "If she hasn't decamped to foreign parts by now, she's probably out there on the streets fighting the revolution. I wouldn't worry about her if I were you. She's not our responsibility. The revolution is bigger than us, remember. It's bigger than her, too. You should be worried about yourself, just as I am worried about myself. Apart from anything else, Adrian, her political engagements are dangerous to me as well. Don't you see that? The whole charade was incredibly fucking stupid on my part. Sooner or later they will come for us simply because we associated with her. Maybe not this year. But next year or the year after that. These people have long, long memories."

I said that that was a trifle cowardly coming from us.

"Cowardly?" he guffawed.

"Shouldn't we be sticking by her?"

"I'm not sure I know what you mean."

I repeated what I had said, and this time around he became exasperated with me.

"She is a charming woman, Adrian. Yes: normally we would, as you put it, be sticking by her. But these are not normal times and the fact is I won't be seeing her again. I'd suggest you do the same, comrade. I can't help it if you disapprove."

Eventually a dessert came which he must've ordered while I was in the bathroom. It was an off-menu special, a pyramid of durian ice cream with lychees stuck into it.

"They bring us dessert," he sighed, spearing a lychee with his fork, "and they call it peace."

WHEN WE CAME BACK up to the street the typhoon had started and umbrellas whirled ownerless down the empty streets. It did not put the slightest dent in Jimmy's good humor, however. He offered me a lift in his limo, but I refused, making the excuse that I had an appointment nearby. In reality I wanted to walk home in the rain and let our conversation sink in and settle down. All along I had had the subtle feeling that Jimmy was lying, both to himself and to me. But I had to ask why. Was he really capable of going so far in iniquity? Perhaps I had felt this ambivalence all along, which was why I had listened so attentively to Bawa in the first place. The Sri Lankan, for all his deviousness, was at least a truthful gossip, and truthful gossip is more salacious than the invented kind. I decided I would go back to him with a bit of inducement and try to get something further out of him. Perhaps I could offer some gossip in return. By the time I had reached North Point I had resolved to talk to Bawa privately and see whether I believed him more or less than I believed the artful Jimmy, even though he was my friend. I climbed the stairs of the Garland up to my overheated rooms, which were filled with exhausted flies, and sprayed them all before sitting down and calling Bawa. But I was unsure what to offer him. In the end, I settled on an expensive lunch on a day of his choosing. He was so cheap, it would get him talking, and that calculation turned out to be accurate. When it comes to free lunches, improbable as it might seem to outsiders, there is a delightful gastronomic dishonor among scribes. Any free spread will get them talking.

EIGHT

I HAD ASKED BAWA TO MEET ME AT FUNG SHING, WITH an air of urgency that would make him react the way I wanted before he had time to up the stakes and bargain with me. As Napoleon once said, *"Vitesse, vitesse, vitesse."* In the event, he was there before me dressed exactly as he had been that night at Spring Deer. The satisfying thought came to me that on his hack wages he possessed only one suit, which he wore on every occasion after ironing it himself under a newspaper. He was ensconced at the table I always took myself; the servers must have directed him knowing that he was there to meet me. Made cognate by despicable foreignness, *gwailo* always hang with *gwailo*.

I knew you'd come around, his smug expression said, and in a way he was right. I had not bitten his bait the first time but now he could see I had gotten hungrier. I ordered my usual dim sum and some pu'er tea.

"Is this your local?" he asked.

"Before you say it, yes, it's a Communist hangout. I come here for the soupy dumplings, not the politics."

"All the same, they must notice you. If I had your politics I wouldn't live around here."

I said I wasn't aware of *having* any politics. "But I know what you mean. You know I can switch to Mandarin whenever I feel like it. I speak it better than Cantonese."

Bawa, who spoke neither, grimaced at the barb. But it wouldn't get in the way of his winning both a free lunch and some information from me.

"We're in the same business, Gyle. I know you know things that you keep to yourself. So do I, so I think we can trade. I trust you to keep it to yourself."

"Likewise."

"We aim to be of service. By the way, you looked rather dashing in those pictures in the *Apple Daily*."

"So you noticed, then?"

"Well, I am one of the five people in the city who know who you are."

The restaurant was in one of its lulls and therefore empty. A perfect place to share secrets. He didn't waste any time asking what I needed or wanted. He was often fond of quoting the Rolling Stones song about needs and wants, to wit, you can't always get what you want, but you can usually get what you need. I think that it was his operational motto.

All right, I thought, let's jump right into it. I asked him bluntly if he knew a girl called Rebecca To. Or even for that matter the To family. He looked up, mildly surprised.

"They're rather for voting rights, aren't they?"

"I'm not sure they are. But even if they are, they keep it to themselves and they certainly don't approve of violence."

"What about the daughter? I don't know her if that's what you're asking."

"But do you know *of* her?"

"Of her?" The surprised look faded slowly and was replaced by something more involuntarily sly. "I won't deny I know *of* her."

"What have you heard?"

"You mean what have I *seen*? The whole city has been talking about her, in case you haven't noticed."

"I know that. But what have you heard about her besides what you've seen in *Apple Daily*?"

"There isn't much to hear. She's a pro-democracy runt, isn't she?"

"So to speak."

He glanced down at his hands, which always appeared to be lightly powdered. And indeed if he had turned up in a powdered wig I would probably not even have blinked.

"Why are you asking?" he said.

"I'm trying to find out where she is. I've been thinking about what you said about Jimmy at the morgue."

His mouth opened as if he was about to laugh, but in the end he was silent.

"I'm wondering if I could find out more about the dead girl there."

"You want to know who it was?"

"Yes."

"Well, you know, Adrian, so would I. It would be an interesting story for me. Why would I give it to you instead of writing it myself?"

"Because I would owe you an enormous favor that you could cash in later."

"Would have to be more than a free lunch, señor."

"We both know the value of it. It might be very useful for

you down the stretch. This is just one story anyway. And do you really want to write it and face the consequences? You might get yourself on the wrong side of the police. About that, I don't care. But you do."

"Obviously I care."

It was the way we hacks often dealt with each other, a cynical interplay of obligations. With a curious elegance he picked out a paper napkin and wrote two names with numbers, as one would jot something down during a bout of absentminded daydreaming. That, he told me, was all I was getting. I could take it or leave it. The slight disdain of this position struck me as being genuine. The names were of employees of the morgue, and I could probably buy them off according to Bawa, though he couldn't say what the going rate was. Nor would they go on the record, obviously.

"I'd ask that you not breathe my name to a living soul," he said, rather redundantly.

"That's the easy part."

He looked at me skeptically and shrugged.

"It's up to you whether you think it's worth it. Why would you want to stick your neck out for this? You're not really going to write something, are you?"

"Maybe it's just to sate my curiosity about an old friend."

"It's usually a bad idea to pursue your own curiosity. What does it have to do with you anyway? I know you and Tang were friends, but that's no reason to jeopardize yourself."

I took a moment to reply to this.

"They're friends of mine, as you say," I said, trying to throw him off the scent. "I didn't know the girl very well. But all the same, she's worth defending."

"From what?"

"That's what I don't know yet. I'm not asking you to speculate, Bawa."

He smiled effortlessly.

"It's usually just smoke and mirrors." He pushed the napkin with its information across the table. "And I fear you wouldn't be defending her."

He poured his tea and seemed momentarily serious.

"I don't want you to write a piece about it, Adrian. It would finish you off. And the gesture would mean nothing, if you want my opinion." He lowered his voice just a degree. "You put too much stress on the word *free* in free press. It's all rigged from the get-go. I've been trying to tell you this for years: the Chinese system is the future. We pretend to write and they pretend to read us. Forget it."

I said, "Then I should get paid is what you're saying?"

"I can't advise you on that. And don't be so sarcastic. I'm just reminding you that you're in China, not the Upper West Side."

"I'm glad to have that insight. But thanks for the tips, Bawa. I owe you. Eat as much abalone as you like."

"I intend to. The dried kind."

The dried kind were four times more expensive than the fresh variety, and he waved a merry hand at the staff.

"*Baa jyu!*"

It was the first Cantonese I had ever heard him speak. Perhaps he got free abalone from other journalists on a regular basis.

He walked with me back toward Java Road afterward and there we stood for a moment, sniffing the air for tear gas and making jokes about it. I disliked him a little bit less after that. We are all in this shit show together, he seemed to be saying between the lines, and there's little point pretending you are more moral than me, or vice versa. He asked me where I lived and I pointed vaguely toward the Garland, which he seemed to know in some way because a pitying look came over his face. The life of the hack is picturesque up to about the age of forty. After that, squalor rears its head.

"Good luck," he said, and left me at the corner of Chun Yeung with an understated finality that suggested we wouldn't be meeting again for a while and that neither of us would mind.

THAT SAME EVENING I called the numbers he had given me and succeeded in getting through to one of them. I opted for my guttural and broken Cantonese in a voicemail to one Dr. Andrew Wong and left a number with him. I told him to think it over and call me, saying merely, "I'll pay well and it's just between you and me."

"What's this about?" Dr. Wong said, by way of a greeting when he called me back.

"It's about a girl who came into the morgue."

I felt cheap saying it so bluntly, but there was no way not to. I wasn't even sure myself what I was asking, I was just throwing darts at a board.

"What girl?"

"Maybe we could get to that when we meet."

He paused for some time, breathing noisily. My voicemail

had clearly taken him by surprise and it was understandable that he would be so hesitant.

"Are you sure that's a good idea? You say you're English. Are you foreign press?"

"Hong Kong press."

"And how do you keep it confidential?"

"I know how to do that. But I'd prefer if we don't talk about it over the phone. Do you want to call me back or shall we make an appointment to meet now?"

He paused. "I'll wait and think about it."

"I'd appreciate it if you didn't mention this to anyone else."

"Very well. I have your word you won't record anything?"

The people who worked in that place would never have heard of me anyway. But a foreigner offering money for a talk was an electrifying dilemma for them, averagely paid as they were.

For the rest of the week I pondered the possible outcome. Wong could easily just tell his superiors and the authorities would try to trace the call back to me. It could happen in a few minutes and then they would be at my door, as they were fond of doing with so many others. Once that happened I would be an enemy of the people and a one-way trip to the airport would ensue. When I thought about it I wasn't too perturbed at the prospect. I would probably lose my apartment and my suits but other men have suffered worse. Yet as it turned out there was no reverse tracing of the call and I realized that Dr. Wong genuinely was thinking it over by himself. Like Bawa, he was out for himself. It meant that eventually he would call back because his curiosity and greed would get the better of him. Sure enough, he did. I suggested we meet at a little café in Causeway Bay where I sometimes went to read. It was a place called Café Corridor that lay at the end of a narrow passageway which gave onto a stairway. The stairs led up to a few ambiguous massage parlors. One could sit there for hours with single-estate French press coffee watching the clientele ascending and descending those stairs, never tiring of the moral confusion written on their faces. Sometimes they stopped inside the cavernous single room for a shot of caffeine after their exertions. I liked it because there were no windows giving onto the street. We wouldn't be observed by anyone from the outside. Any such person would have to come down the passageway and be seen as they entered the Munchkin doorway of the café itself. There were only five tables.

Dr. Wong himself was painfully obvious when he did appear in this way, a man of about thirty-five in a gray linen T-shirt and jeans looking a little conspicuously off-duty. It's curious how people who have made a rendezvous without knowing each other will recognize the other almost immediately. There is a flash of guilt between them.

I got up to shake his hand because I needed him to like me a little and he had done nothing wrong, after all. He was not the enemy.

"Do you really speak Cantonese?" he said in that language, incredulous but hoping it was true.

"We'll have to switch to English. Do you mind?"

"I'm a doctor. I speak it, too."

He sat down and I thanked him for putting himself out. It was also an apology.

"I've put you in an awkward position."

"You have."

But he smiled weakly and his fear came out in that same smile.

"It can't be helped. But it's for a good cause."

"I thought it might be. But I'm helping you for the money. I don't care about your cause."

I had gathered together two thousand USD and slipped it inside an envelope, which I now pushed over to his side of the table. It wasn't much for a Hong Kong doctor but I was banking on a moral dimension to his anonymous whistle-blowing. That was my gamble. The money was merely a token gesture. I was relieved, therefore, when he took it calmly and I told him how much it was. It was not as much as he'd hoped, perhaps, but if that was the case he didn't reveal his disappointment. And I realized that I had been correct to assume that moral dimension. He simply asked me what I wanted to know.

"It's about one of the young people who came into the morgue."

He pointed out, with some weariness, that a number had shown up over the last few weeks. There were always suicides. Now, however, there appeared to be a surge of them. I asked him how big the increase was. It was hard to say. He shrugged. He wasn't a statistician. Some were as young as fifteen, mainly girls. But that group was often the majority of suicides, even in normal times. The older men in dire financial straits were always there, too. In a city of high-rises it was probably the easiest way to end your life, easier than many other methods. Very few people shot themselves in the head, because guns were so hard to acquire.

"My friend told me that a girl had arrived at the morgue and that a quite-well-known man had come down to identify her."

"Yes, I remember that."

"Was that man Jimmy Tang?"

"I wasn't involved directly. I think one of the other doctors said it was—"

"Did you know of him beforehand?"

"Vaguely."

He said he couldn't be one hundred percent sure it had been Mr. Tang. It was only one of his colleagues who had asserted it.

I said, "And why would Mr. Tang have been called down there by the police?"

"I couldn't say."

"Then who was the girl?"

I was getting close to my reason for bribing him and he squirmed a little in his chair. Plausibly he could deny knowing. But he could sense that I wouldn't be satisfied with that and might ask for some of the money back. Then he did something strange. He picked up a sachet of sugar from the table, opened it, and spilled the contents over the surface between us. Then he drew a Chinese character in the sugar with his index finger. I saw at once that it was the character for the To family name. It was a shock without being a surprise. I leaned back, however, momentarily out of breath, and something inside me gave way and the muscles of my back went slack. He reached out and wiped the character away so that the silent message was erased for good. His eyes were blank because it meant little to him.

I asked him bluntly what they had done with the body. He said that it had been taken away for disposal. In Hong Kong, that meant cremation. Had the family been notified?

"It's the normal procedure."

"I suppose the parents came down to the morgue as well, then?"

"That I couldn't say."

I felt the blood hammering inside my temples and for a few moments I was unable to get my breathing back to its usual rhythm.

"Are you all right?" he was forced to say, looking at me with a frown of concern. He was a doctor, after all.

"It's nothing," I said, running a hand over my brow.

"Was she a friend of yours?"

I shook my head, though I watched as the doctor scrutinized me even further for a moment.

"Come to think of it," he went on, "your face looks familiar. Do I know you from somewhere?"

"It's unlikely."

But his eyes had finally come alive. Yes, he had at last recalled the tabloid picture and in his mind, I could see, it was all coming together. I was the third figure in the scandal. Maybe you should be paying me to keep silent rather than to talk, those same eyes now said. But who was I, really? He turned coquettish.

"Aren't you afraid I'll take your money and turn you in?"

I said I wasn't a Chinese or Hong Kong citizen so being

turned in, as he put it, did not represent quite the same risk that it would for a Hong Konger. It was a bluff on my part, but it seemed to work.

"It would be bribery," he said archly.

"I'll say it was a misunderstanding."

He was not as docile as he looked, then.

"Tell me more about the girl," I said, beginning to sweat and lose control of my hands. "There's no hurry. Go ahead."

I ordered more coffee. He talked quite smoothly. The girl was a drowning. She had been taken into the lab and they had examined her. She had been dead for only two or three hours and in the water for just an hour, and by way of explanation the police had told them that she had been found at the surface floating a half-mile out between Waterfall Bay and Pak Kok Tsui. She was partially clothed but wearing only underwear from the waist down. He was not, however, the one who had completed the autopsy. That was another doctor. But later that man had told him privately that although she had drowned, it was very possible she had also been assaulted beforehand. This doctor was sure that she had been made unconscious before being left in the water. Her blood contained traces of droperidol. It was a strange agent to find in her because it was usually used for its anxiolytic properties. However, high doses made it useful as a sedative for terminally ill patients when one wanted to quell their delirium. It must have been used to sedate her, because the concentrations in her blood were remarkably high. The colleague on duty at the morgue told him that he had been instructed to fill out the forms indicating suicide as the cause of death and to leave it at that. It was presumably why Wong had been withdrawn from the autopsy; they didn't want any dissenting opinions. Wong's colleague had filled out the forms and signed them, because at the end of the day who doesn't want to live a quiet life? Afterward the colleague had told Wong what he really thought in order to get it off his chest. But then again, she had hardly been the first they had seen or the first about which they had heard rumors. As far as the two doctors were concerned they were protesters being picked up every night and taken to high-security depots. What happened inside these holding facilities they couldn't say. His colleague didn't much care, but he, Wong, did care. He was not political, he said, but he cared.

I sensed then that he had spoken to me for reasons other than just money. He might not care about my "cause," but his conscience was bothering him. Was that it? So he was not as cynical as I had initially assumed. Maybe things got a little frenzied, he went on, and maybe the police didn't mind it that way. It enabled them to vent their frustrations. Either way, it was hardly random. The word was that they were arresting the students and "picking out" those they regarded as the bad apples because they already had files on all of them. Therefore they knew exactly who the girl was and why she was on the street. Where she had been picked up, he couldn't say. But, I pressed him, why on earth would Jimmy Tang have been called down to the morgue before anyone else?

He stammered, "I-I can't offer you a theory, I'm afraid. Maybe his family have an understanding with the police and they wanted to keep him in the loop or out of the tabloids. You know how this city is."

"It's the only thing I do know, I suppose."

The pieces had begun to come together in my own mind. Terrible Tang had been called to the morgue by the police, whom he obviously knew well, before news of the girl's death got out. His involvement made no sense until I thought about it a bit more. Was it possible that he had been involved in her disappearance? He had certainly gotten rid of an embarrassment, a thorn in his side. Maybe he had done it under the guise of an accidental death at the hands of the police during a confrontation. It was extravagant to think it might be true, but in the end it would have been convenient for him.

I thought back to our conversation at Mott 32, his hint that she had wanted to blackmail him. I didn't believe it then, and nor, I thought, did he. But now I began to entertain the possibility that I might have been wrong. Confusion began to well up around and within me. It was a bewilderment deepened by the dissolution going on all around us. You could say that the whole society had become paranoid as it swayed on its no-longer-solid foundations and began to disintegrate. Therefore I, and everyone else, would become paranoid as well. Nor would Jimmy's paranoia be exceptional. It was the new reality and we were all in it together. Whatever still existed of the boundaries between the police, the government, the powerful families, and the media seemed to have been removed from one month to the next. The old Hong Kong of laws and judges in British wigs had been deconstructed overnight and in its place there had emerged a wild twilight totalitarian world in which rumor, hyperbole, hatred, tribalism, and supposition were regnant. Now, when a crime happened—say, when a student protester was found drowned in the sea or dead from an apparent suicidal jump from a tall building—no one could assume that they knew what had really happened. If it was a genuine suicide, no one believed it; if it wasn't, much of the population did believe it. Insinuations and gossip sprang to life around the event. It was impossible to know who was telling the truth. Whether it was the police or the tabloids, we all told stories to explain the event to ourselves. No one knew what was solid and what was air. Suspicion was the only governing law of the new age. How could it have been otherwise when the entire state was now built on secrecy and dissimulation? So a society melts away, like something solid, as I had also thought before in the bathroom at Mott 32, vanishing into thin air.

In any case, Wong went on, after these odd events with Jimmy Tang neither he nor the other doctor had been allowed back into the lab for a few hours, and when they had returned to work the following day the body was gone. The disappearance was as complete as it was enigmatic. He looked at me and there was a faint, slightly cruel smile. For a while, then, he and I drank our coffee without talking further. I felt exhausted and I suspected he did as well.

I told him I would leave first and that since we should not be seen together he should remain with his coffee for at least fifteen minutes. I gave him one last eye-to-eye and went out into the street as if in need of moral fresh air. Think about a man who needs to be paid to divulge what he knows to be criminal. On one level, it wasn't his fault—he was in an ambiguous position. The rebels called them *gong zyu*, timid "pigs" who prized their everyday lives over anything else, but I couldn't blame them, given that they had their own families to feed. I think often of those middle-class professionals living under Mao in the Jiangxi Soviet of the 1930s who were assassinated to cow the population and whose wives and children afterward had to roam the streets for years as beggars. No one ever knew what became of them. Wong was in the same position as those men had been, and it was better for his children if he talked only to me and preferably for a sum of money. It was easy to despise him, but as I walked back to Java Road I realized I didn't feel superior to him at all. There was, after all, something vaguely noble in his corruption.

NINE

AS JIMMY HIMSELF HAD TAUGHT ME AT UNIVERSITY through Izaak Walton, the compleat angler was a master of feints and maneuvers. Through the grapevine I heard that he was still throwing his weekend parties at Borrett Mansions and that the journalists who had once attended them had gradually been weeded out. This included myself, though I was in fact grateful for the exclusion. It was Cunningham who told me. But why, I asked myself, did I have to hear it from him? I could just as easily go to Borrett Mansions myself and force the issue. Rather than call in advance and be turned away politely, I drove up there one night in a taxi and asked the driver to wait for me in the driveway outside the same doors where Jimmy and I had stood with our cigars just a few short weeks before.

The old concierge was still there, but with a blanket thrown over his shoulders. He recognized me so felt no need to call up to the Tang apartment, therefore I went up unannounced. It was a dangerous move, but I could always say that I was passing by and had wanted to see them. Nevertheless I hovered outside the walnut door and strained to hear anything from inside. It was quiet. I stepped to one side so that anyone peering through the viewer would not see me, and rang the bell.

There is a certain kind of silence that is the sign of panic. Something moved, then stilled itself. I rang again. Curiosity always wins out. Socked footfalls approached, very quietly, and I could sense the eye behind the peephole staring out into the landing. Then the door opened and Melissa's voice came onto the landing and asked who was there. I stepped out, as nonchalantly as possible, and made the grin sheepish. "You!" she gasped and, not hesitating too much, slid off the chain and stepped out onto the landing with me. She was in house slippers and sweatpants and a cashmere cardigan that didn't cover her chilled and goosebumped arms. The first thing she said was that Jimmy was not there, he had gone on a business trip to the U.S. and would not be back for a few days.

"I was passing through," I offered by way of petition. "I thought—"

"You didn't think to call?"

"I did, but Jimmy didn't pick up—never picks up, in fact. So strange."

"Would you like to come in, then?"

The offer was unenthusiastic, but it would be worse for appearances if she simply refused to let me in.

"Just for a minute," I said. "Since I'm here."

"Yes, since you're here. I think you also owe me an explanation. Don't you?"

"I do, yes."

The admission seemed to satisfy her.

I saw at once that the apartment was shut down in some way. The furniture was draped with protective dust sheets, the carpets had been rolled up, and one of the Murano chandeliers had been dismantled, lowered to the floor, and wrapped.

"End of the season?" I wanted to quip, knowing that there were no seasons and if they were wrapping up their chandeliers they were moving on to somewhere else for a while. It looked like Jimmy had made good on his offer of moving them to America. I took a look around as Melissa made us tea in the equally bare kitchen. On the terrace the view looked more sinister, the lights more symbolic of some vague pandemonium and malice. As of last night, she said, Jimmy was in Los Angeles buying them a new house. They already had a place in London. But Los Angeles, to them, felt closer, on the Pacific Rim where they belonged. I said that I understood, though privately I was taken aback. Could that be true? I scanned the walls for the artworks and saw that they had all disappeared. Perhaps it was true, then. After my interview with Wong, in fact, it felt all the more likely. That he had not told me was indicative of his guilt, since otherwise he would have dropped me a note before skipping town. She sat with me, haggard and drawn, her eyes filled with strain and exhaustion. It was very different from the last time I had seen her.

"I assume you wanted to talk to Jimmy about something."

"I did. It's related to what we talked about last time I was here. But since he's not here and you are—well, I'll be honest with you."

It struck me that she had been in need of a confidant for a long time and in some curious way I had promised to fulfill that role for her. Not that we ever got down to brass tacks when we chatted together. All too obviously, my role had now been subverted by my complicity with a wandering husband and it could never be restored. Still, she wanted to know things from me that only I could provide.

"We know her family socially, Jimmy and I. That was what was so shocking. An affair with her, of all people? My father wanted to have him arrested."

"What for?"

Her eyes narrowed. "How old is she? Twenty-three or something? What a fool Jimmy is. And you for going along with it and then having the gall to show your face here."

She was speaking her mind but I could see her anger was tinged with possible forgiveness down the line. She knew I was not as bad as her husband.

I said, "He invited me to go on the yacht for the day. It was after you and I had spoken. I didn't know she would be there."

"Didn't you?"

"He didn't say anything beforehand."

"You never were a very good liar, Adrian. You're one of those men who lie because they think it's honorable, and then do it badly. Which is dishonorable."

"I promise you—"

"Don't promise anything. I don't want to hear it. You're a prick, Adrian. But since you're here, I suppose I have to offer you a drink." Her manners were as rigid and impeccable as she was.

She got up and went to their luxurious cabinet. It was the temple of Jimmy's alcoholic fantasias.

"What would you like?"

"Whisky and ice," I said.

"You're very undemanding about your liquor. I like that. It's your best trait."

They had an old-fashioned soda fountain of ruby glass and the sound was comforting to the ear. She walked back with two whisky sodas and handed one to me, having ignored my request for ice. Her mind was elsewhere.

Back in her velvet throne she asked me sarcastically what toast Jimmy and I liked to raise when we were alone.

"Who's better than us!" she echoed, and raised her glass.

It was Jimmy's whisky, an old Brora. You couldn't find it now. It was his toast, too.

"It's surprising you came," she said. "I'm even surprised you've stuck by Jimmy all these years. I'm not sure he's the loyal type deep down. He hasn't ditched you, that's true, but then he hasn't needed to. If he needed to, he would. He ditched the girl, didn't he?"

"He said he did."

"In a funny way I feel sorry for her. Do you know where she is now?"

I lied and said I did not, but there was something off-kilter about the way she asked it, as if she already knew the answer and was playing the game.

She said, "What was your impression of her?"

I paused for a long time. "I don't know what to say. I didn't talk that much with her."

"I think I met her once myself when she was much younger. It's pretty vile, Jimmy would've met her then, too.

I'm assuming, Adrian, you had nothing to do with those pictures coming out in the press?"

"You have my word."

"For what it's worth, I believe you. My father is smoothing it over behind the scenes. She is apparently some kind of activist in the protest movement. Did you know that?"

"I doubt it's true."

"She is a *jung mou,* a frontline fighter. My father is apoplectic. It's a threat to the whole family's relationship with the Chinese state. I can't believe you didn't realize that, getting on that yacht with them."

I said nothing to that.

"I'm curious as to what you're going to do next. You're not in a British outpost anymore. And you know Jimmy is counting on your loyalty from now on, don't you? I've always counted on your discretion and you've always delivered. You lied to me about that girl, but it was for Jimmy, so I understand. Well, I try to."

She took a large gulp of her whisky soda and looked around the living room. I asked her when they were leaving.

"We're still deciding it. I want to go to Italy for a month first. I feel like he owes me that, at least. I intend to clean out his bank account."

But, I thought, you'll return to Hong Kong soon enough. You're tied to this city by the heartstrings.

Then I said, "Did Jimmy never say anything to you about where Rebecca is now? You must be curious yourself."

"Why should I care about that little whore? I hope they tear-gas her every day for the rest of her life."

"Jimmy didn't say?"

"No. Naturally, I've asked him. But he said he has no idea. For once I believe him. And you don't know either?"

I shook my head, and I had the sense that she was not being entirely truthful. And so in those moments our mutual regrets moved below us, water under the bridge, then quickly passing out of sight, and I was left wondering whether I really knew her at all, even if I had always known she wore a mask with me. Exasperated, I got up with a frivolous show of formality and said I'd better be on my way, but she herself remained seated, still glacial and coldly furious.

"Tell me, what is she like?"

I had to think while I pulled together a quote that would serve.

"She's—lively."

"Lively?"

She sneered and looked at me as if I were joking at her expense.

"Is that all you can come up with?"

"I don't know—she's a cockroach, as you would say. A *gaat ʒaat*. A beautiful cockroach. I think Jimmy was a little in love with her."

It was the cruelest thing I could say to her but it made her relent and the sneer left her eyes because it rang true. The sudden deadness in her face released me and I quietly said my goodbyes and went out alone, back to the landing and the Art Deco elevator. Yet again I was reminded why they call us foreigners ghosts, *gwai*. We have no substance in their social order. I had never had that word *gwailo*—the word *lo*, or man simply added to it—tossed in my face up till then but I often wondered when it would happen. Even as an insult it might have some truth to it. On my longest nights, I had often dreamed of dying in a hospital here then waking up and walking back to my prior life, not realizing that I was no longer real. A common nightmare among the aging. You walk down a sunlit street at noon and suddenly you perceive that you cast no shadow on the sidewalk.

TEN

NEVER FOUND OUT IF JIMMY HAD REALLY GONE TO Los Angeles on his business trip or whether he had in fact been listening to us from one of his closed-off bedrooms. Everything about the Tangs became more obscure by the day. Despite what Melissa had said it was now impossible to be friends with them since, as far as she was concerned, I was an accomplice to their scandal, however much she had hinted that she might forgive me. That said, his little scandal came and went and, as if the fickleness of the collective mind were at play, Rebecca To's name also came and went, brushed off into the shadows where many people felt it belonged. Aside from her parents and friends, it was I who was left with the question of her disappearance as something experienced night and day, an emptiness that felt like a great slow-motion decay in the heart. Guilt played its part. We had not known each other very long, or very deeply, but I felt that my silence had helped cover up her erasure, and again I had willingly played my role of accomplice.

It was the cleanliness of this erasure that surprised me the most, though I couldn't say why I should have been surprised. No formal announcement of her death appeared, the

To family made no grieving proclamation. The reason for this, I theorized, was that they had elected to keep things quiet and not draw unwanted attention to themselves. They had kept their grief private as well. It must have been an extraordinarily difficult thing for a Hong Kong family to do, and it would have been against all their ingrained social conventions. But the times were no longer ordinary and people had changed their behaviors accordingly. People have endured more extreme distortions of their customs in more violent societies and so their secrecy did not seem entirely impossible to understand.

But the effect was as if she had never existed. This calamitous idea grew within me over the following days, so that eventually I began to walk all the way down Java Road in the afternoons to visit the funeral parlors that famously crowd the sidewalks toward its lower end. I went to look for Rebecca among the funeral portraits. I knew perfectly well that her family would not post her image there, but something irrational drew me anyway.

The biggest of these was the Hong Kong Funeral Home, the principal venue for wakes on Hong Kong Island. I had been there many times as a society reporter and recalled yet again the death of Leslie Cheung, whose wake had also been held there in far happier, distant times when it was singers and movie stars who caused grief when they threw themselves off buildings and not the maddened students with nothing to lose. I had passed by just to have a look—many of us were sent down there to cover it—and yet had never gone inside where the crowds of fans had gathered. I could not believe at the time that the star of *Nomad*, perhaps the biggest

star in the Chinese world at that moment, had hurled himself
from the top of a hotel. It had felt like the end of a cultural
era. I thought about it as I walked along the length of Java
Road; 2003 now felt like a century ago. Could one imagine
today a Chinese actor naming himself after Leslie Howard,
that epitome of British sangfroid and mellow elegance? "I
never did anything wrong in my life," Cheung had lamented
in his brief suicide note. "Why does it have to be this way?"
And who knew the answer to that question?

I came to the first of the smaller parlors that line one side
of the street with their bouquets laid out on the sidewalk.
The Hong Kong Funeral Home stood as Java Road's terminus, a curved building with cream ceramic walls and a railed-
in sidewalk usually littered with the chopped-up stalks of
flowers and remains of bouquets. The curved black lintels of
the doors set within gold columns bore Chinese characters in
gold and beyond them all was somnolent and hushed.

Though it looked like a humdrum office block from the
outside, the Home enjoyed a certain reputation. The famous
liked to have their last rites there. Society personalities, as I
had noticed, often made their last stop on earth within its
premises, and you might say that it was quite the place to be
seen *for the last time*. At the hour of my arrival, however, it
was not busy. I slipped inside unnoticed and went unhope-
fully from room to room, for some last vestige of Rebecca,
knowing very well that I was never going to find her. There
had most likely been a quiet cremation, at the discretion of a
weary family. The Tos had made a resolution to keep it out
of the news. What I could not understand, though, was the
indifference of my fellow hacks. For them, too, a thousand

other stories were more pressing and took up all their time. It was impossible for them to cover them all, so they showed no interest in it whatsoever. And so this one had passed them by without their feeling obligated to dig deeper. Of course it was also possible that they had avoided it at all costs. Either fear or indifference had them in its grip, it was hard to say which.

As I went from floor to floor, from wake to wake, I realized that I was alone pursuing a chimera. The dead woman's ghost was watching me from afar. I believed in it. She, too, was now a *gwai*. As such, I felt her in the environment around me, a spirit in its discontent, vocal and tangible only inside my own mind but challenging me directly. Through sheer misfortune, I was seemingly the only witness to her disappearance willing or able to do something about it, the only one apart from my source who did not have a vested interest in minimizing it.

In Chinese mythology ghosts who have not received justice return to earth to seek vengeance. They are either "hungry" or "wandering" ghosts. Offerings are made to them. They have to be appeased, laid to rest. At the Festival of Hungry Ghosts on the fifteenth night of the seventh month offerings are made to them. There are nine kinds of hungry ghosts, but I could only guess as to which category she might now belong. But then, what about the living? Rebecca might have had friends who wondered about her, who had gone looking for her, but I knew none of them. Nor did any of them contact me. We moved in different circles. And so we were an anomaly, I and Rebecca's ghost, alone together. On Java Road, among the funeral parlors, this became quite clear. As I passed banks of flowers and black ribbons on the sidewalks, I knew that I was being followed. The feeling persisted the farther along Java Road I went, and soon I began to stop, turn, and look back into the waves of faces coming toward me, faces that were now more alien to me, just as I was to them.

For a while I found myself passing between sheer walls of concrete and glass with the loading bays of small businesses open to the street and palettes strewn across the sidewalks. It was, I think, not far from Technology Plaza. I stopped with a sudden exhaustion, an emptying-out of the lungs, and paused to let the sweat on my legs dry off. I had already forgotten what time it was. Late in a stale muggy afternoon, the light dimming into dusk. I looked behind me and across the street to a high pale pink condo building and there, caught in the shade cast by a truck being loaded by several men, I saw a woman walking peaceably by herself and hugging the pink wall. For a moment I was sure that it was Rebecca, glimpsed as she moved between parked trucks but unmistakably her.

I crossed the street quickly and pushed through the other pedestrians to get a better look at her. However, she had melted away. Either she had stepped into the condo building or she had crossed the street herself but in the opposite direction. I called her name, sharply so that heads turned. There were so many small trucks loading and unloading that if she had been there she could easily have slipped away without her even noticing me. Getting no reply from anyone, I went back to where I had been standing originally and, not knowing what else to do, asked some of the workers if they had seen someone adhering to her description. I drew nothing but blank looks. I ran up to Harbour Plaza and frantically began looking through the columned arcade that gave onto King's Road where the tram lines curve around. I followed them just as a tram rolled up, and I was seized by the idea that she might have gone to the Healthy Street East stop in order to take the tram. When I got there the tram had stopped and people were getting on and off. For a moment I saw her again, getting into the car, and I was fast enough to catch the same tram before it moved off toward North Point.

I edged my way through the car looking for her but by the time we were at Healthy Street West, the next stop, I still hadn't found her. The crowd was too dense, unwilling to part for me.

I therefore stood by the windows waiting. Tin Chiu Street came and went. Then, at the Shu Kuk stop, she got off and went up King's Road until she had darted into the crowds milling around the Sunbeam Theatre buying tickets for that evening's Cantonese opera.

Of course, the Sunbeam. As we had discussed at the China Club that night, the Sunbeam was one of the last nooks of old Hong Kong; that evening's opera, no doubt filled with flying ghosts, was a place I should have taken her—or vice versa— had we been allowed to get to know each other in other circumstances. But it was there I lost her, not able to see whether she had gone into the theater or had simply moved through the crowd and exited on the far side. I lingered by the ticket machine outside, a bright red contraption in the form of an old-style weighing machine with a five-HK-dollar coin slot. Engraved metal text in Chinese read, "When the wheel stops you can insert a coin." People were weighing themselves as the machine spat out tickets, and I thought it probable that she had done the same and then gone inside. I hesitated, wondering if I should weigh myself and pay the five dollars, but in the end I did. I sweated my way up the stairs past walls of photographs of stars in '60s bob cuts, blinded by the huge overhead bulbs, and so into the suffocating dark of the theater itself, where a performance was already under way. There was no possible way to see her there but I waited for an intermission and watched the opera—a stage filled with red candles and entwined trees with paper flowers and a girl in a towering headdress of red silk intoning words that I could just catch: *tonight petals are falling, obscuring the moon.* Indeed, paper petals were falling from the rafters. A ghost would naturally return to its previous haunts, as we all know.

I walked home afterward and the streets had cleared early. At the Garland the foot-massage floor was plunged in darkness and the building's internal corridors had acquired a new quality of silence, yet on my way up I heard the TV sets and the drains working quietly as normal. I lay down on my sofa and thought it over. It was inconclusive. It had been her, there was no mistaking her, yet she could not have disappeared so completely anywhere except the interior of the Sunbeam Theatre. I should have waited and flushed her out, but I had not. Now there was no way to find her a second time.

These thoughts, though, were themselves absurd, since it could not have been her and I must—I knew in my rational mind—have been pursuing a mirage. The funeral parlors and their heartbreaking kitsch had gotten to me. I went to the computer awhile later with a glass of Hibiki and opened it up determined to email Strick back with some notes about an idea I now had to write something about the recent disappearance of students, and of course Rebecca chief among them. How, I would ask, could people just disappear, people with no reason to vanish of their own accord? I thought perhaps, with a few leads, I could persuade him to give me some time to write it and in fact it had been forming in my mind for some time, this idea—a denunciation, a j'accuse aimed at the whole system, a hypothesis about Rebecca's death written as a thinly veiled denunciation of Jimmy himself.

There must be such a thing as synchronicity, coincidences which we feel cannot be entirely accidental. Seeming connections between events that are either delusional or in fact have been arranged by supernatural forces. In my emails just at that very junction I saw a message from a correspondent I didn't recognize, the sender's name written in Chinese characters. *Phoenix*. It had a file attached to it. My immediate thought was that someone was reading my mind. Or a spirit was reading it from afar. The email contained no message, but the file encoded in Microsoft Word had the same name as the sender. When I opened the file the screen went dark and there was just the text, which was written in Chinese and began, "*I, Rebecca To*—"

I leaned back with a little heart-stop. It was a prank, surely. But if it was a trolling hate mail, it was well done. I could imagine the troll department of the state sending it to try to cow me; it was something they could and would do. All the same, I began to read it.

What followed was an account of my evening with Rebecca at the China Club, something only she and I would

know. Or else state intelligence had been spying on us. Whoever was writing the document recounted the circumstances
of Rebecca's death. Rounded up, taken in for questioning,
assaulted, drugged, taken out to the harbor for disposal. It
was not unlike what I had suspected, but here all the details
were present. The writer described the doctors at the morgue,
which could not have been possible, and I recognized the figure of Dr. Wong who had so chivalrously taken my money.
Then the interiors of the To family house on the other side of
the island, which I had never visited but which seemed real in
this account. There was Jimmy and there was me. There was
the Cococabana restaurant on Shek O beach and the lighthouse at Cape D'Aguilar, the upstairs room at Duddell's, the
swim at the rocks, and Tom, the skipper of Jimmy's yacht.
Rebecca might have divulged all this to a confidant, though it
was remarkably complete, too complete to be likely. It had
even recalled the conversation we had had while we were on
the rocks during the boat trip. Jimmy calling over, "You look
like seals—seals with brains and sunburn." How would a
person who had not been there recall something like that?
Yet all the same I thought back: the girl at Duddell's that
night, though I couldn't remember her name. Kerry some-
body. Then the name drifted back to me, Kerry Hui. It was
not impossible that Rebecca had related all these things to
her, even including Jimmy's asinine one-liners.

Someone watching quietly from the sidelines, from the
shadows, and those ten pages could have been a message in a
bottle from her. They were also a gift to me personally. There
was another possibility, however: that one of her comrades
had sent it to me anonymously. For that matter it was possi-

ble that this person had written it, too. It could be someone
who knew what had happened and who wanted me to get it
out to the wider world, sending the email as a prompt. There
was an implicit permission for me to use this narrative and
publish it as insider information, not unlike the techniques of
underground propaganda in wartime occupations. The back-
bone of the piece I was considering had formed itself instantly: I could send it on and have it published without
embellishing at all. It would be fictional in the eyes of readers, but it would also be read as factual—it would be my version of "The Melon of Huangtai." This, in the end, was what
I proposed to Strick. I sent him the email in its entirety, asking him what he thought of it, and he responded by pointing
out something quite obvious: that a shadowy unnamed male
lover depicted in the email as being complicit in the girl's
death was possibly, even probably, Jimmy Tang. If he had
jumped to that conclusion, so would everyone else.

To this I replied that I could write a piece that would
imply an unnatural death in which Jimmy had been complicit, just as the email suggested, though obviously I could
not know how or why and I would leave it to the reader to
make that connection. It wouldn't exactly be what Strick had
been expecting. But it would be a political statement. I would
be explicitly ratting out an old friend with an accusation that
was all hearsay and suspicion—precisely the mode of
thought that the new order made dominant. There would be
no evidence behind it because we no longer lived in a world
of evidence. It would be *samizdat*—underground resistance
literature from Soviet times—a word meaning "self-
published."

Strick at first was doubtful.

"But it's just interpretation and animosity," he said coolly. "You are not, Adrian, a disinterested party."

"So what?"

"Is it what you believe?"

"It's my gut feeling. That's all."

"Normally I would be careful with a gut feeling. You've been quite distraught and under the weather lately, what with your attack in the street and all. Are you sure?"

I said I didn't care about anything anymore. I wanted to go out on my shield.

"What shield?" He laughed.

"That's my whole point. Now I have the shield."

He took some persuading but gradually came around. It would be libel, slander if I even suggested the name of Jimmy Tang, but if I wanted to he was prepared to weather the storm—up to a point. And then it was I who hesitated. It would be a bold thing to do, given that I had no evidence apart from a hunch and a few dubious sources. But the whole point of going out on your shield was that you believed in the fight, no matter what you could prove in a court of law. Besides, what court of law even existed now?

FOR A WHILE I stayed locked up inside the Garland living off deliveries. When I was bored I went to Fung Shing for the soupy dumplings and watched violence in the streets on the restaurant television along with the Fujianese motherlanders. Crowds of black-clad youth came surging along streets, countered by men in white throwing traffic cones at them and brandishing homemade clubs. Each side, no doubt, thought of themselves as patriots. It reminded me of a quote by the great Italian writer Ennio Flaiano: "In Italy we have two kinds of fascism. On the one hand there is fascism, and on the other hand there is anti-fascism." Yet I was feeling more gifted with a purpose. Soon I sent the reworked pages of my narrative to *The Raven* and was surprised that Strick was impressed by them. We discussed how to present it.

Would it be my voice, Rebecca's imaginary voice, or an anonymous source, he posited. In the end we went with an anonymous source and put it in the third person. We called the source Phoenix. I insisted on it because I knew Jimmy would get the reference at once and I wanted it to wound him, to make him bleed, and to give him sleepless nights. The piece implied that he had helped cover up her death in circumstances that were deliberately wrapped in the utmost ambiguity. The reading public already knew of their romantic association. Now more layers of conspiracy would be laid over a mere episode of adultery. I was not accusing him of murder, only of cowardice and expediency. But that was in some ways equivalent. Strick gave it the green light.

For several days after the piece came out I watched it catch fire on social media, creating a maelstrom of rumors, and simultaneously and without any fuss I went to ground as quietly as I could and continued to watch the scandal grow. Even without my name attached to the article, those who made it their business to know such things could make the connections easily enough. They would know within hours that a filthy *gwailo* had made it all up to smear the Hong Kong

Police Force. For what does a totalizing state not know? It was time to vanish.

The Garland itself had grown moribund as it sank into its own defensiveness. As the streets became unsafe people instead gathered inside and whispered together in the corridors adjoining the stairwell. I could hear them, even late at night, the gossip urgent but also edged with a jovial confidence that the speakers were on the right side of the state in the long run. Pro-Party gang members staying there after they had been bused in from the mainland? It was possible that some of them had been assigned the task of keeping an eye on the journalist foreigner. Long past midnight, when I was still working, I heard slippered feet moving past my door, taking their time. Bugs could be mounted anywhere. They could be fixed to electrical wires, to door frames, to the insides of drains. The whole structure could be a honeycombed listening device, for all that I could ever know. At the same time the transient population that I suspected had moved in to the Garland had become more vocal. Voices speaking in Mandarin, men talking about "chases" and "skirmishes" as they moved up the stairs, gathered on the landings with a bottle or two, laughing among themselves. Just as the city was changing, the Garland was changing hands. And day by day the story of Rebecca To grew on the internet until it had metastasized into a string of conspiracy theories that flashed continuously through the electronic synapses of the city. The police vigorously denied; politicians evoked the CIA agent who had scripted the defamation. And all the while I only wondered what Mr. and Mrs. To thought of it.

The meeting with them that I had been dreading finally came about, though not because of any initiative on my part. It was just a normal afternoon as I was walking down Java Road when I felt over my shoulder a car shadowing me at a crawl and I realized the To clan had finally found me. It all happened as smoothly and unremarkably as a random encounter in the street, which it was not. My only surprise was not that they had tried to find me, and succeeded, but that they had taken so long to do so.

ELEVEN

THE CAR STOPPED JUST AHEAD OF ME AND A DRIVER IN full uniform jumped out with surprising friendliness and announced his master's name. Would I mind taking a short drive with Mr. To, since he would greatly appreciate a conversation with me, if I didn't mind? After a moment's alarm, I consented. Despite my shock I was in fact eager to talk to him. He was enthroned in the back seat of his ancient black Daimler with tinted windows dressed in a plum corduroy suit and matching suede loafers with long black Bresciani socks. He apologized for having followed me, then shook my hand with a strange withering smile and asked the driver to lock the doors. For our security, his tone seemed to imply.

"Shall we drive around, Mr. Gyle? I can let you out wherever you like. I even have some whisky in the car," he said, pointing to a small walnut cabinet set into the partition before us. Its door was spring-loaded and formed a tray with tumbler holders when opened. "What happened to your face?"

By now I had almost forgotten my wound, as if it had happened long ago, in another century. Reflexively, I reached up to touch it, assuring myself that it was still there and had not healed.

"Oh, this. I hit a door."

"Good for you. At least you don't get into fights like some people I know. Do you take ice in your poison?"

"One cube."

We drove out toward the Chai Wan Gap and To asked me to tell him a bit about myself. I seemed to know a lot of well-connected people in Hong Kong. Was it a scheme of mine?

"To do what?"

"You journalists—you get around. I suppose you know all about the To family." We were in sight of the moonlit sea and he pointed at the shadowy land mass on the far side, the mountains, which always look improbably unattainable and distant, and I wondered if he actually remembered that we had almost met that night at the China Club. The night I had walked through the park with his daughter.

"We came from over there, like everyone. My grandfather was a black marketeer. It wasn't so long ago. We were friends with the British, though. Are you a homesick type or a lifetime expat type?"

"I'm an immigrant, so the latter."

"So we're both immigrants in a way. Immigrants or emigrants. You strike me as more of an exile. The voluntary kind. It's a happy destiny in some ways. I always say it could have been worse. One could have been left behind."

I asked him if he wanted to talk to me about Rebecca since, I added, he must have seen the photographs of me with her and Jimmy.

"Photos?"

"Am I wrong to say that?"

He looked cold and stricken but he did not seem hostile to me. On the contrary, it seemed he had persuaded himself that I had nothing to do with her death. No, he admitted, it was not wrong.

I said I was sorry, more sorry than I could say over a tumbler of whisky in a moving car.

"She might," I said, "have been in the wrong place at the wrong time."

My words were rational enough but his face had become tortured and dark, the lips running away with themselves a little, as if they couldn't catch up with the thoughts moving through his mind.

"Isn't that what they always say? But it was a curious day, the day that she disappeared. The thunderstorm."

"What day was that?"

"I think," he said, "that you remember that as well as I do. We both know."

It was a curious thing to say, I thought.

The night I saw you all together at the China Club? I suggested, as delicately as I could, that it was possible that I had seen her with them at the China Club on the night in question. Was I mistaken?

"The China Club?"

He was genuinely taken aback, and denied having been there with Rebecca.

"But," I said, "you *were* at the China Club?"

"What do you mean? We go there almost every night."

"Ah, I see. But when were you last there with Rebecca?"

His look grew more perplexed.

"We've never eaten there with her. She detests the place."

I stayed calm and tried to jog his memory.

"It must have been an occasion that's slipped your mind," I tried. "You can recall it if you try—"

"I recall *everything*, Mr. Gyle. My wife and I eat there to be alone. We don't even dine with friends. Rebecca, not at all. As I say, we've never once eaten with her there except a Christmas dinner three years ago. Now, that I do remember."

"I-I must have been mistaken," I stammered.

"You were there?"

"I go there often enough. I'm a member."

"I've never seen you there. But may I ask, how did you know it was us in the dining room? We've never been introduced."

Yet my mind was racing backward in time, to the gimlets, the odd shine of her skin, her lipstick that left no mark on the rim of her glass. I had seen them all together, I was certain of it. I had taken Rebecca's hand for a moment as we stood up from the bar and it had been as real as nightmares ever are. Everything had seemed solid and brilliant—enlivening, even—and yet all those physical things might have not been real after all. Had I even been there the way that I thought I had been? How real had the walk in the park been, the taxi ride up the mountain in the dark?

"In any case," To went on, keen to move the conversation away from the China Club, "I've been meaning to have this talk with you, Gyle. I know very well that you and Rebecca were friends, and the three of you were on that yacht together. I found out, too, that Jimmy Tang is an old friend of yours. In the light of that, I wondered—we wondered, my wife and I—if you had anything to tell us about our daughter's death. Or else if you know they were having an affair."

"I know that Jimmy Tang went to the morgue. And yes, they were having an affair."

"Are you sure about both of those things?"

I said I was as sure I could be. His hands tensed as if they were pulling at a mental rope and his eyes turned venomous.

"That vermin. That *leper*."

He seemed to be responding to both pieces of information at the same time. He pressed me about their relationship and I told him what I knew, which was a fair amount.

"Rebecca and I were not close friends. Still—I feel I ought to tell you that. In case you thought I was holding it back."

"We have the gravest suspicions about Mr. Tang, I must tell you. And he has been behaving strangely. He hasn't come to see us. He won't even admit he was involved with her. He's a coward, isn't he?"

Aren't we all? I thought.

"He's running from something," I said. "He's afraid."

To then relaxed his hands and a more resigned mood appeared to come over him. It was useless to keep talking about the slippery Jimmy. He said he had been feeling the presence of his daughter over the preceding nights; he could not sleep and the great trees around their house seemed unusually disturbed by winds. The security lights kept coming on for no reason, the chains at the gate rattled. His wife told him that Rebecca's spirit was near them, she could feel it, too, and was certain of it. She was stalking the house and letting them know that she was there.

Did I believe in ghosts, he asked. I said I wasn't sure how much I believed in them. "Ah," he sighed, "you're not Chinese." For them, he said, it was quite otherwise. Then he asked me if I thought his wife was well advised to seek out the medium she liked to visit in order to talk to her ancestors. I said that I couldn't offer an opinion on that either but perhaps it had an alleviating effect on her emotionally.

"Do you believe in it?" he said.

"In mediums? Not at all. Do you?"

He was already looking placidly through his tinted window.

"Of course I do. What do you think?"

He meant that for him such things were not a matter of conjecture. They were as real as cement walls. But I wonder if Jimmy does, I thought to myself.

"Where do you stand on that, Mr. Gyle?"

I said I stood on the side of science, of course, but that science didn't know everything.

"But in any case," he said, "who thinks about science when they're mourning?"

By now we had reached Chai Wan and were circling past Cheerful Garden, the towers of this Alphaville set against storm clouds, the endlessly monotonous curve of Siu Sai Wan Road perfectly serving the purpose of such a conversation. We came to a spacious junction framed by skyscrapers and at the far end of the road ahead of us the mountains reappeared, soaring up into the underbelly of the clouds. There were no pedestrians and very few cars. To, as if thinking aloud, said that he had been meaning to ask a thousand things of me. Now that I had told him about Jimmy's presence at the morgue and the affair between him and his daughter, he found himself somewhat numbed and bewildered.

"How do you know the Tangs?" I asked, trying to rekindle the conversation. To shook his head gravely. "I've known his family for decades. I can't stand them. His father is not too rotten, though. Believe it or not I used to go trout fishing with the man in Scotland when we were young. He used to talk nonsense about fishing as if it were a philosophy. I never knew what to say. Fishing may be many things but it is *not* a philosophy. It's a dumb sport. Enjoyable but dumb. No doubt his idiot son thinks it's a philosophy, and you probably do as well."

"I did when I was twenty."

"It's dumb even for a boy of twenty. As for Jimmy, I've met him many times since he was a child. He was always a fairly arrogant boy. I always thought he was careless with others."

"You mean he loses them like children lose toys?"

"That's certainly one way of putting it."

He poured me a second glass and there was a fatalistic melancholy in the fumbling gestures of his hands as he picked up the in-car ice bucket. He told me about his visits to his friends in the upper echelons of the police as he had tried to glean some information about what had happened to his daughter. For years he had been dealing with politicians, with Beijing investors, with Party princes for whom he had arranged the sale of valuable properties through his family connections. And what he had learned was that they always managed to, as he put it, "silence the frogs." It was a reference to the security details assigned to Chairman Mao's fifty villas in the 1950s. Each villa was located in a scenic rural area and many of them were equipped with underground railway links, bombproof shelters, and bulletproof arcades where the Chairman could take his constitutionals without exposing himself to sniper bullets. The master of the nation lived like a prisoner inside his own vast state machinery, eternally fearful of assassination or rebellion. In his villas he could swim in heated pools and enjoy the prized live fish from distant provinces brought in from the four corners of the land in plastic bags on special trains to be served at his dinner table. But one thing he could not control. He disliked obtrusive noises of any kind, especially those of dogs and frogs. The security details were charged with noise suppression. The dogs were easy to kill off, but the frogs presented a more obdurate challenge. They were too small and too numerous to shoot. At length the security details suggested to the Chairman that they should use dynamite to exterminate all the frogs within earshot of whatever villa he was staying in. History does not reliably record whether this method of quelling the frogs was ever effective, but Mr. To assumed that it had been. It was both easier and more difficult to silence frogs than it was to silence human beings. The only complication with humans was a logistical one: how to gather them all in one place so that they could be dynamited. Obviously it was impossible. But the theory at least was in place. As long as the theory is there, the practice will follow sooner or later.

"You mean I'm a frog?" I said.

"At least you're small. You can hide."

Like a grimly tarnished Cinderella I had now been

whisked back to my point of origin at the Garland and, as we drew up under the neon feet and the images of heat-soaked women, the rear door opened automatically.

"It's been a sad meeting," To said, shaking my hand for a final time. "I hope you'll understand that we won't be crossing paths again. My wife sends her regards and asks me to thank you. She says you're an educated man. Even if you are a friend of Jimmy Tang I'm not sure *educated* is quite the quality one needs these days. *Zoi gin*, Mr. Gyle. If I were you I would get on a plane to London as soon as you can."

"Why?"

"Hong Kong is no longer safe for any of you."

"You're the second person this week who has said that to me."

"Nor will I be the last. But will you listen to the advice? Probably not. You're a Hong Kong lifer, aren't you? A dying breed. The last of your species. Well, it's up to you how you roll your dice."

THE DAYS BECAME COOLER and more solitary. Sometimes I took a cab up to the Peak and walked along the Victorian promenade suspended above the rain forest and stopped to look at the To family mansion immersed in its India rubber trees. There was not a sign of life, just like when I had walked Rebecca home. If I was forced to leave Hong Kong in the near future this quiet spot would be the place I would miss the most. It was here one afternoon that I stood by the railings with a few elderly Chinese tourists watching a column of black smoke rising from one of the universities in Tsim

Sha Tsui across the harbor where a battle between occupying students and riot police was going on. Above us, disturbing that otherwise uneventful autumn day, helicopters turned in circles, the faint thud of the blades reaching us even on the Peak, and I considered how curious it was that the empty To mansion was a perfect viewpoint from which to observe the spectacle, day and night. I stayed there all afternoon watching it, and by the time I had reached the cable car sailing back to Wan Chai I felt as if I had drunk from the cool and deep well of Rebecca's childhood. Not only that, however: it was part of my own past as well—the parties on the Peak, the cocaine marathons on the balconies of houses whose owners I could no longer remember, the innocent optimism of the days just after the Handover.

TWELVE

WITHOUT DEATH," MAO USED TO SAY, "HUMAN LIFE could not exist." As an aphorism justifying the 35 million deaths during the Great Famine I've always thought this saying possessed a remarkable, no doubt psychopathic coolness of touch. But like many of the Chairman's sayings, it meant nothing at all when you mulled it over for a few seconds. The same was true of his sayings about cities, of ways of life; about books, culture, and for that matter whole civilizations. They were worthless. When intellectuals, that hopeless tribe, objected to his destruction of irreplaceable ancient sites across the country he cleverly made them part of the demolition crews. There was nothing he hated more than Chinese architecture. However, he seemed to love poetry, which he wrote himself. Inevitably, then, into those ensuing weeks of limbo, I thought about the Chairman and Rebecca cremated out of sight and then poured as ashes into a plastic container.

I heard some days later that the Tos had boarded up their house in Repulse Bay and decamped to London in time for Christmas. The Tangs had gone to ground. Jimmy never called me once after the anonymous "Death of Rebecca To" hit the Hong Kong airwaves. He must have been stunned. He knew it had come from me, it would not be something he wouldn't understand at once. Strick, true to his word, had to let me go in order to protect his precious *Raven* and ensured that I would be paid for three months by way of a modest severance. I didn't have any hard feelings about it. For the first time I was retired with a wage. I could float away from my previous life.

The protests went on, but they no longer gripped me. I knew how they would end. The state rarely loses such combats. Journalism, at the same time, was a young man's game, as I never ceased to repeat to whoever would listen, and it was anyone's guess what an older man's game actually was. Gardening and equally aging wines? I looked around me yet again. A way of life was disappearing rapidly and therefore (not being in any way exceptional) I was bound to disappear with it. I recalled that the Chairman, looking out one day over the once variegated and historically rich skyline of Beijing, still intricate and infused with Buddhist meaning, remarked that he could not wait for the day when, looking out over this same enchanted view, he would be able to admire instead a vast field of chimneys. He got his wish.

AT FUNG SHING A few days after the Western calendar New Year, during a quiet week, I ordered my usual and sat at my corner table until the early evening, when I would walk home. It was there in the only restaurant I still frequented, that Mr. Meat Cleaver Li, the man with the red face and the Fujian accent, spotted me from across the room one early evening midweek and let out a roar of laughter that turned all heads in the dining room. He was among a raucous group drinking beers and shots of *moutai*—there was a bottle of treasonous Kaoliang from Taiwan on the table, and it must have already worked its insidious magic upon them by the looks of their sweating faces. Mr. Li shouted out a few jokes and stabbed the air and then turned his gaze upon the ghost on the opposite side of the room. I heard my name, *Ah di le an*. The recognition had surprised them and then delighted them. But how, I wondered, had they recognized me at all? Who had given them my name and an image of my face, and why? A wild idea formed: that the security forces had got wind that I was the author of the libelous article directed at their honor, the honor of their marvelous police force and of the government that controlled it. So, my fellow diners seemed to be ruminating, that traitorous author was the man who had been coming every day to their turf for years, and yet they had never known! The waitresses, caught in this strange moment, shot anxious glances in my direction, but for a different reason. I realized that it was fear for my safety, and by extension the reputation of the establishment.

The laughter became louder and with it the jibes in Fujianese accents directed obliquely at me. I called over my waitress and asked for the bill. Before it arrived, however, Mr. Li staggered drunkenly to his feet and lurched across the room toward me carrying a teapot in one hand. He came up to my table and loudly demanded to know my name. He knew that I spoke Cantonese, he shouted, so there was no use pretending. I didn't know what he wanted or why he was annoyed with me, but then again it was possible he had heard from the staff that I was an unworthy foreigner who had insulted the hardworking and patriotic officers of the law. I told him in that language that I was about to pay my bill and leave. At this he took the lid from the pot and hurled it at my head, though it grazed my shoulder on its way to the wall behind me, where it ricocheted to the floor. The table of men from which he had come burst into laughter again. It was an encouragement, an incitement to go further. Lifting the pot of tea, he grinned for a moment and then emptied the scalding contents over my head as I made an attempt to get to my feet.

My arm deflected the pot itself but the tea burned my face and blinded me before the waitresses could throw themselves between us. The pandemonium that erupted was strangely muted and soon it had become a silent dance, the enraged Mr. Li, the waitresses, the other diners recoiling, and at its center me, stumbling toward the light from the windows with an unused napkin in one hand. The staff sat me down and the insane one was bundled out of the restaurant by the manager before the police arrived, if they would ever arrive. Instead an ambulance was called and the manager put ice on my face while we waited for the paramedics to appear. Out on Java Road the attacker lingered with his friends, cackling and shouting until they were persuaded to disperse into the evening. Minutes later an ambulance came to take me back to Canossa, a hospital, it seemed, I was doomed to never abandon.

THE BURNS WERE NOT severe but I stayed the night at Canossa all the same since they had also detected some ab-

normalities in my heart rate. Seated upright in a bed with a
view that my insurance paid for, and calmed by Ultracet, I
was unable to sleep, though in a way I enjoyed the isolation.
I watched the Hong Kong news on the room's monitor and
waited for someone to call—anyone, just a voice of consola-
tion or support. None came. Either they had not heard about
the attack or they considered it prudent to give me a wide
berth for the time being. My handful of old friends would
probably wait awhile before bringing the limp flowers. I had
a feeling that many of them suspected it was I who had written the story of Rebecca's death.

In the end it was Cunningham who brought the flowers
and condolences. He came into the room darkened with rain,
dressed in an old Burberry that looked as if it was far older
than he was, and gave me the bundle of books he had brought.
One of them was Ha Jin's work on the bard, *The Banished
Immortal*, which I had already read but was still glad to see. I
was disappointed to see no oranges or chocolates, however.
He did bring me some multivitamins along with some com-
mentary on the outside world.

"Your story is still being talked about after all this time"
was the first thing he said as he drew up a chair next to the
bed and brought into my orbit his ahistorical scent of long-
digested single malt. "You are the hero of the hour. Freedom,
democracy, and facial burns. I'm surprised no one has been
here to see you."

I already knew some of this, of course. But it was satisfying to hear it from a human being, face-to-face. I said that it
was early days in the repression and that a year from then, or

two years, I would not be lying there unmolested. Besides, they could not care less what foreigners said or thought for the moment. It wasn't white privilege; it was contempt.

"You've had it easy, then."

"I've been feeling very peaceful in here. I hope they forget the hero stuff by the time I get out."

"Well, speaking of that, there is other news."

And I realized then that he had not come to bring me books and multivitamins but to relay this other news.

"It's about your friend Jimmy. Someone attacked him outside his house. The two of you seem to be in synchronicity."

I was not only surprised but, in some unpleasant way, rather pleased.

"Is he all right?"

"He's not badly injured."

"So we were both assaulted in the same week?"

"It's peculiar, isn't it? I don't know if it's that serious but it seems a girl followed him home and stabbed him in the leg with a penknife." This salacious item had been kept from the main news outlets and had surfaced only via Twitter, he said.

"It's hardly believable," I said.

"Nevertheless it happened. Stabbed him right in the knee."

"Is he crippled?"

"You sound like you're hoping for it."

A crippled Jimmy, it was a fine idea.

"Who was it?"

"Some girl from here."

"I don't suppose they have a name?"

"Kerry Hui. Mean anything to you?"

I had to smile and then refuse to explain why. The ever enigmatic Kerry Hui again. Vendettas were occurring all around us as the city descended into disorder and so it was not entirely surprising that after my article had been published someone would go after Jimmy, just as the men at Fung Shing had gone after me. But there was no point in talking about this with Cunningham. He was one of those reporters who made it his business to go to the sites of suicides and record every detail as if he were making catalogs for posterity. He had to believe those suicides were perfectly normal or he would lose his mind. Perhaps he had already lost it. In his earnest way he now wanted to know what I intended to do with myself. It was obvious to him that I couldn't stay in Hong Kong since I was now identified to the authorities as a meddlesome *gwailo* who had insouciantly and groundlessly denigrated the honor of their policemen. A whole lifetime of my grubby literary service had been for nothing, with the exception of my grand parting shot, my final fusillade.

"You really did yourself in, Gyle, if you don't mind my saying." He launched a playful punch to my arm and winked. "Any job openings in London these days?"

"Failed in Hong Kong, try London."

"That's pretty much what it is these days. Or just retire to Kingston upon Thames. It's what I'll do eventually."

And so it was the moment for the well-rehearsed ruminations on the setting suns of the disappearing world order and our uncertain place within it. "The last of the colonials," he said, handing me a multivitamin with a glass of hospital orange juice. "If you leave now, in six months' time no one will remember your name. If you're lucky."

"Twenty years for nada."

"That's the way it is. The ones throwing themselves off balconies are the lucky ones."

"They're hopeless. Wouldn't it be better to die on the streets using catapults?"

"To what end? It's for nothing. We're the new Tibet."

"Except that Tibetans don't have British passports."

"They wouldn't want them," he said.

"I've thought about opening a hotel in Bali," I countered. "I mean, to hell with Kingston upon Thames."

"Me, too. I think Bali might make me untouchable."

"By whom?"

"The British tax man, obviously."

He finally pulled a mini bottle of scotch from his pocket.

"Let's have a wee fucking dram and toast the end of the world. The berks and the bell-ends are in charge now."

I wondered how I would translate this British slang into Chinese if I had to. There was no way I could. Li Bai would be easy compared with that.

"If we come back in ten years," he said, "all the streets will be named after the Comintern."

"I doubt it."

He poured out two measures in plastic hospital cups and I made a toast to our inglorious pasts.

"Who's better than us?" I said, raising my glass. I thought of Jimmy then, and how twisted that same toast had become in my own mouth.

Later I reflected on the possibility that his words had unconsciously persuaded me to do just that, to leave. The burns on my face healed and became smooth and slightly luminous, like pebbles worn by winds, and from then on I was like a man marked by the signs of his own sins whenever I walked down a street. The curious thing was that I didn't mind. It seemed deserved. I hadn't thrown myself from a balcony or been taken from life during a night in summer by men who would never face a sentence. Why shouldn't I carry a scar right there on my face, alongside the other one caused by a well-aimed left hook?

The poet Li Bai, I often thought, had been the same, wandering across Tang China from household to household, temple to temple, searching for refuge, job opportunities, saints, fellow poets, solitude, and haphazard inspirations. Nothing is more famous than this: *I lift my head to look at the moon, I bow my head and think of home*. I had asked the nurses to lend me a pencil and paper and I used them to do a few more translations from one of the books Cunningham had brought me to kill the nights. Even the above words could be shuffled about and rendered in different ways. *Ju tou wang ming yue*, "raise head watch bright moon," could be turned into a different music if you had a whole night in which to do it.

THIRTEEN

FTER I HAD RETURNED TO THE GARLAND TO BEGIN my recuperation I lay in bed reading Basho. Poetry, in the end, was not enough but at the same time I envied an aging and depressed Basho walking alone through medieval Japan along the dangerous Edo Five Routes. In the end you walk the roads and then die in a simple hut, like Basho. I took to going back to the Vic and its rooftop pool and there spending my afternoons reading the papers with a gin and tonic. There were worse ways to spin out the days. The staff had gradually become used to me again and inquired after my health as if I had been absent on a long trip. On the roof one could be alone in sun and humidity, within the glare of the sea, with only a few businessmen and ambiguous girls silently arrayed on the loungers. Basho, I thought, would have approved because from this vantage point one could also observe the rising moon at cocktail hour.

It was then that I took on the idea of impulsively escaping the city for a while, disappearing without a trail but without resorting to the airport, which makes everyone conspicuous. I thought of Lantau Island. When I was younger, in fact, I would often retreat to Lantau and the Tai O Heritage, a for-

mer British police station converted into a hotel, which over-
looked the sea at the village of the same name. I would go
there with of-the-moment girlfriends or books and sometimes, rarely, both; and as I grew older I would occasionally
go with neither. It reminded me of happier times. Times that
now felt as if they lay outside of history altogether.

The Heritage lay on the edge of the island, with somber
jade mountains on the water opposite it, its rooms painted
white, many with original fireplaces and French windows.
Since there were only nine rooms its privacy was unmatched.
I would know every other person there at any given moment. Moreover, there was no road running past it, just a
footpath that ended in a jetty where ferries once used to stop.
There I could take my coffee every morning and sit with my
legs dangling over the waves.

Surrounded by the ocean on three sides I could feel removed from the threat of interlopers from Hong Kong. I cal-
culated that the crisis had depressed the hotel industry and I
was right. When I got there the Heritage was empty, the
mountains over the water were darkened by clouds, and the
small hill of tropical forest where the hotel stood was hushed.
They gave me the room I had taken with girlfriends in years
past and there I slept for twelve hours a day. When the rain
swept in I sat on one of the patios and read the books I had
brought with me, four Conrad novels arranged chronologi-
cally. I watched everyone who passed on the path below and
everyone strolling on the jetty, and kept a keen eye out especially for the private boats that sometimes drew up. I told the
staff that I was taking no calls or visitors. Not that I was expecting any.

The promenade in front of the hotel, with its row of black iron posts and its open view of the Lantau peaks, was my daily walk as I went into Tai O. It passed under lovely old trees that must have been planted by my countrymen in centuries past. It resembled the path around the Peak that Rebecca and I had walked together. A landscape nudged into a different shape by a race from the opposite side of the earth. But as the path left this manicured zone it seemed to pass back into China, with the tackle and plastic pots the local fishermen laid out along the shore, the Shaolin Wushu Culture Centre behind a circumference of half-hearted barbed wire, the cement structures with faded red Chinese characters, and the watchful stone lions everywhere. Soon there were shops with pieces of butchered fish hung in rows and flower stalls set against the water amid stacks of baskets. By the estuary the houses were on stilts, above the mud with strange homemade chimneys and banner flags.

Here, days quickly turned into weeks and, as my stay became longer, I came to know every inch of this passeggiata. I would stop by the mudflats at low tide and smoke for a while, content to be surrounded by nothing but old people and birds pecking their way across the mud. On the balconies of the two-story houses behind me old men lay on ruined sofas smoking as well—it was a harmony of ancient and contemplative smokers. I avoided the main village farther on, as it was often crowded with day-trippers from the city on weekends. From the mudflats I would turn and walk back to the Heritage, unnoticed despite my race. One afternoon when I arrived there, however, the rain had just started to fall when, as if knowing that I was approaching, one of the staff from the hotel came down to the footpath with an umbrella for me. He handed it over and said that a private boat had just pulled up at the jetty and that perhaps I was expecting a visitor?

"I'm not expecting any visitors here," I said, wanly.

"Yes, we know. All the same—there's someone here to see you."

I told him that I would go down to the jetty myself to see who it was. If it was the police it would be better to be done out there where no one would notice. So I walked to the jetty under the hotel umbrella and as I reached the first of the steps leading down to the water I saw the launch heaving against the tires and the shine of an ice bucket resting on a table at the rear. I knew then exactly who it was and, unsurprisingly, the figure who had disembarked only a few moments before was now standing at the far end of the jetty alone in a pale green Bruton fedora. The one man who I always thought would show up sooner or later.

NOT ONLY THAT, BUT he implicitly forced me to walk all the way to the end of the jetty to meet him. As if it were I who should displace myself to find him, and not the other way around. How typical it was; a meeting conducted via our old patterns. I made the sea trip, he seemed to be suggesting, so you can endure the short walk.

He was dressed in a gray Prince of Wales suit with beautifully ancient black oxfords. When I reached him he turned quietly, aware of me already. So there you are, you rascal, his look seemed to say. Then without acrimony Jimmy held out a hand to shake and gave me a once-over, as if I had gone to

seed but he was too well-mannered to make a point of saying so.

"Are you hiding out, Adrian?"

"I'm taking a few weeks off."

"Aren't we all? I've just gotten back. My father-in-law insisted I get out for a while. Quite a spot you've got here."

"It's not really mine."

"Quite so, quite so. But still, I can see why you're here."

I suggested that we go inside since it was raining and he
was without an umbrella, but he didn't seem put out by the
drops spotting the surface of his suit.

"As a matter of fact," he said, "I made a dinner reserva-
tion for us up at the hotel. I hope that's all right."

I stared at him. "Are you sure that's a good idea?"

It didn't need to be said that this was why he had come out
to see me. But it hung in the air so obviously between us that
Jimmy turned at last to what we were both thinking.

"We both have things to feel resentful about. Let's bury
the hatchet for the sake of dinner, shall we? For what it's
worth, I have the impression that the brouhaha is dying down
a bit. It always does. People always find something else to
obsess about, idiots that they are."

"If they didn't we wouldn't have anything to write about."

"Speaking of which—you know," he went on, not looking at me but instead gazing out over the rainy mountains
and their rolling mists, "I don't blame you for writing that
drivel. Pretending you had some sort of inside information
about her death. The market, so to speak, demanded it. Don't
protest, you know what I mean. Your profession is even
more corrupt than mine. We both know it. We're all whores,

you and me, everyone. But in the end, I understand. You misunderstood the situation because you didn't ask me directly and then you jumped down the rabbit hole of your own conspiracy theory. For Christ's sake. You were upset."

"So you are saying I was wrong all along?"

"Of course you were wrong. You were played by some sharp players, that's all. You shouldn't have been so desperate for the scoop."

"Desperation has nothing to do with it—"

"Well, it wasn't animus against me, was it?"

This I denied, but at the same time I was forced to wonder if there wasn't a grain of truth in it all the same. If it was partially true, why did I resent him anyway? It wasn't just about Rebecca, surely. It came also from our own past—the way I had come to be able to see through him, to make him transparent without him realizing it. For, after all, this was what he had always been able to do to me. When we were young, he was always in the superior position, always able to judge my vulgarities and mistakes. That's one thing our unconscious never forgets or forgives. The question is only whether as one grows older success, money, and fulfilled ambitions enable one to forget it. But I pretended otherwise.

"Of course not. I followed the evidence."

He turned finally, brushed the rain from his shoulders, and tried the old smile, comfortable as a pair of kid gloves one has been wearing for years.

"It could be argued, comrade, that that was the one thing you didn't do. You didn't have any evidence at all."

I could have argued, but I knew in advance how useless it would turn out to be, how impossible it would be for him to admit that he had done anything outside the invisible laws of power and wealth. He would deny everything I had heard from my sources, whom of course I had indeed paid and who, it occurred to me dismally as we walked slowly up to the hotel, might well have been lying all along. If, as I had admitted to myself, it was impossible to trust anyone or their stories in a city made totalitarian, why should I have trusted them? Who was to say they hadn't just taken the money and the little favors and the free lunches and had a quiet laugh at my expense? They wouldn't have cared one way or the other.

Even later into our meal, seated under the restaurant's glass roof with the rain drumming upon it, I could not broach the subject in any detail without him turning on the reproach again. This was now, I understood, his line. I had savagely wronged him and he had come there to squeeze an apology out of me. Apart from anything else, he said, honor demanded that he establish his innocence in my eyes. He couldn't let something like that go.

As we walked over to the hotel, I had noticed the limp with which he was afflicted, I hoped only temporarily, I had said. He'd grimaced and waved a hand. At dinner, though, he opened up about it over the second bottle of red. Some crazed friend of Rebecca's had taken it into her head to strike a posthumous blow for the honor of her friend. He had been stalked. Rueful was all that he felt about it now. He even knew the girl, her name was Kerry, he said. I understood at once that he had completely forgotten that I had met her at Duddell's, if briefly. But there was little point in mentioning the fact.

"Stabbed in the leg?"

"With a goddamned penknife. I didn't used to think those kids were terrorists, but now I've rather changed my mind. She staked out my place and waited for me outside the garage. I couldn't have seen it coming. Anyway, I assume you heard all about it."

"It'll be on your tombstone."

He topped up our glasses in lieu of an absent waiter. Or perhaps, I thought, he had paid them to leave the room.

"The blade went right through the tendons. It was a miracle I can still walk. I had to spend a week in bed."

"Did they catch her straightaway?"

"They didn't catch her at all. She took the next flight out of town and went underground."

"Then how—"

"That's the crazy thing. Kerry wrote me a letter accusing me of being involved in Rebecca's death. It quoted your article. I'm not saying it's your fault that I got myself stabbed, of course, though I *am* saying that it's your fault. She's a young hothead and she believes everything she reads. She's just an idiot. But *you*. Melissa wanted to sue you, or worse. But, what can I say, we're old friends at the end of the day. Anyway, it would only magnify the scandal and would serve no purpose. So we decided to let it go. As for Kerry, I didn't ask the police to go after her. It would only have made matters worse and anyway I'm exhausted all around. What's a little crippledom here and there? My doctors say it will improve over time, unless it doesn't. But I see you've had quite a bit of violence thrown your way as well."

I had quite forgotten about my scars created by the burns, but now that it was brought up I said that I no longer nursed the vanity of my younger years.

"Better that way," he said, raising his half-useless leg.

When Jimmy's charm came into play I found it hard to completely disbelieve him, and in any case how could I be sure one way or the other? There was always a zone of doubt and confusion when listening to his tales. And of course there was my own excitable state, which had led him to find me here, on the edge of an island, seeking solace and repair, though I didn't want to acknowledge it. I had gone through a period of storm and shipwreck. I thought back to the sighting of Rebecca on the tram on King's Road. Pure fever, surely. I would never really know what Jimmy had done or had not done, for only he could really know and he was never going to tell me. But I pushed back anyway.

"You didn't tell me what actually happened. You didn't even answer your bloody phone."

"It's true, I went shark hunting."

It was his tired old phrase for going on the lam.

"I called you over and over," I said. "You could have just explained yourself."

"There was nothing to explain. I knew nothing about Rebecca's death. Nothing at all. Why did you assume otherwise?"

I said I had my reasons and I left it at that. I wasn't going to tell him that I thought intuitions had come my way through channels I could not rationally explain. But he went on anyway:

"What you forgot, *tongzhie*, is that many people hate or

envy me and want to see me brought down. You might have
brought *that* into consideration. Melissa for one insists that
we sever contact from this moment hence. She says it's es-
sential if I'm to survive. I think she's right, I'm sorry to say.
If anyone ever saw us together they'd draw some crazy con-
clusions. We have to make this the last supper, as it were."

"I'm surprised we're even having one."

The mood had been growing tenser since I had met him
on the jetty, and now the unspoken resentments found their
moment to be spoken. But strangely, it was he who volun-
teered his while I held mine closer to my chest because I
knew how futile it would be to accuse him. And so it was he
who spluttered and felt the blood rise into his face.

"I should be furious with you. I should have had you
court-martialed and shot. It's a strange thing, decades of
friendship, and you go and pull a traitor move like that. What
the fuck were you thinking?"

I let this little hypocritical storm burst over me and then
pass on. Our friendship, I saw then, was not one written in
some permanent medium. It was like a million others whose
history can't be reliably remembered. Something light as a
spiderweb, complex, but easily broken by a touch of jealousy.

I wasn't yet sure if I had made a mistake, or whether he
was just turning on the bluster and bluff so that we could part
ways without him admitting to being an accessory to a killing. Such things mattered. They were points of pride. What
hardly mattered to him was whether he was in fact in the
wrong or in the right: it was a question of face. We might
meet again one day years in the future and he would want to
glance at me for a moment and not feel that he was losing

face. Reputation was the one thing that he possessed and that, when it came down to it, he could defend with a certain amount of savagery.

Even then, at the moment when we were emptying our last bottle of wine together, and the unbidden nostalgia of the years swept back upon us for the last time, I knew that he was lying and that he didn't care if I knew it. What if he's telling the truth and he had nothing to do with Rebecca's death, I thought. Was it even possible? But glossing over the agony of this unresolved question we talked with a false pretense of calm about the past, slipping further away from us with every encounter, and he talked about his memory of me at twenty—as if it were his duty to remember it because nobody else could or would.

"When I first met you, you were lying in that scraggy field by the river at King's, I was with Emily Chen. Do you remember her? She said, 'There's a homeless person on the lawn. How did he get in? They certainly aren't shy, are they?' It made me laugh at the time. Did you hear us laughing?"

"No."

"It's just as well. What snobs we were, Emily and I. She died in a car crash in Portugal in 1997. So much for that. The next time I saw you, you were walking through the courtyard at Clare carrying your copy of T. S. Eliot's essays. It was so . . . *studenty*. And you carried that book around with you everywhere for a year."

"At least," I said, "I wasn't wearing New and Lingwood boating blazers."

"Fair point. Was I?"

"You absolutely were."

"Must I plead guilty to one thing, then?"

"You must."

He raised his glass, the bad wine trickling down to the base of his wrist and the band of his impeccable watch, and there was a sort of love in his unstable eyes, which the alcohol had already detached from any common sense.

"I apologize for the blazers. It was a sincere mistake. But I was thinking the other night—does *Ah di le an* still read T. S. Eliot's essays in bed at night?"

"I've become more populist. Now I just flick through the Drudge Report."

It was clear he didn't know what that was and so he went on without even a smile.

"We were better then, weren't we? Who was it who said if you want to know how you've done in life tell your eighteen-year-old self in the mirror whether you have disappointed him or lived up to his expectations."

"It's not a conversation I'd want to have."

The room then seemed to grow darker in my eyes, and the slight movements of the staff to disturb a sadder vacuity. It was like a restaurant to which no one will ever return, a place existing purely to accommodate our final parting. Empty tables with marigolds shone with their useless cutlery and untainted glasses. He talked a little more but I found I was no longer listening to him. The curtains were coming down on our association of decades. I thought back to Cambridge, summer nights at the Eagle or walking through the courts of St. John's, where he had once stopped me as we were crossing the bridge together and told me to observe the perfect moon at that moment reflected in the river below. A Li Bai moment if ever there was one, he was quick to point out. The poet had fallen drunk into a river in the year 762 while captivated by a lunar reflection, hoping to grasp it. But it was also a moment to remember *The Compleat Angler*, in which it is written, "As no man is born an artist, so no man is born an angler." Over the years Jimmy had certainly made himself into an accomplished—a complete—angler. He knew how to wait, to make his move when silence had overcome and lulled his prey. He had become what his father had always wanted him to become, while I had become someone who would have been unrecognizable to my father. This was what our ever-diverging fates implied.

Afterward I walked him back to the waiting boat, the rain having stopped and the clouds having parted as they do in this part of the world, suddenly and without warning, replacing one mood with another in the space of a few minutes. His limping leg dragged slightly on the paving stones and threw his hips out of rhythm. Seeing us, a man in uniform jumped up from the launch and climbed the steps to offer his arm. Jimmy told him he was all right and that he wanted a few moments alone with his friend.

We strolled to the end of the jetty, where we had stood before. By now a half-moon glittered on the sea and we could hear birds from far away, excited by something on the shore opposite us. He put his hand on my shoulder for a moment and asked me to keep everything we had said between ourselves. Unto death. But the tone was light and resigned. For a moment I felt as if I would seize his hand and squeeze it until the pain shot into him, maybe flip him into the water below. But the moment passed.

"I suppose this is it, then, comrade," he said, holding out his hand. "I hope you return to London. This is no place for a gentle soul like you, and perhaps you've served your time."

At that last moment I realized it was too late to ask him whether Rebecca had died accidentally or if there had been a design behind it. Not his design necessarily, but a design all the time. But I knew he would not speculate even to me. Why would he? He had already said that it had had nothing to do with him. Reading this impasse between us, he turned without a further word and strode back to the man in white, who rather feudally was holding out a heated and rolled wet towel on a silver dish. As the launch pulled out from the jetty and into open sea, he raised a glass to me from the gloom of the deck shining with polished brass and I caught a faint whiff of music, an old song of Roman Tam if I was not mistaken. As I walked back to the Heritage I found to my surprise that I even knew the words.

FOURTEEN

IT WAS MANY YEARS UNTIL I SAW JIMMY AGAIN. MY London life, when I rejoined it, was exactly as I had imagined, only worse. I bought a small studio in Battersea and made peace with the idea of living a life as different from my Hong Kong one as I could stomach. There was the problem of growing old as well. Except that I didn't experience it as a problem. I still had my W. W. Chan suits and my dictionaries and I now had time to complete the translation of "The Exile's Letter," that fever dream devoted to the mysteries of friendship. I had enough funds to get by and from time to time I was invited to give those lectures at the National Liberal Club that I had always meant to deliver.

But my life was still just as indistinct. I took to making nostalgic day trips. From Battersea I walked across Chelsea Bridge to Victoria and took the local Brighton train, as I used to do as a child with my father. Now I would go down as far as Hassocks and then return without leaving the station, passing over the viaduct at Balcombe and staring down at the fields and hedgerows that had once been mine but which now represented a past even more completely lost than the landscapes of Hong Kong. Even here there was nothing to hold on to. After an absence of three decades no one I knew lived there anymore. I was as much of a *gwailo* here as I was in North Point. I would never have expected to find "The Exile's Letter" to be so true to my own life as it now became, but perhaps I should have expected it. Walking back across Chelsea Bridge after nightfall on my return home I became lost in the kind of reverie that I had managed to avoid for most of my adult life. The bridge of St. John's under the same moon during the first term when I was struggling with these lines:

> *Till we had nothing but thoughts and memories*
> *   between us.*
> *And when separation had come to its worst*
> *We met, and traveled together into Sen-Go*
> *Through all the thirty-six folds of the turning*
> *   and twisting waters;*
> *Into a valley of a thousand bright flowers . . .*

In the end neither Jimmy nor I had been able to improve on that for the simple reason that nobody had ever been able to. So it transpired that the only thing that I had truly enjoyed in the intellectual domain of my life had turned out to be the thing at which I had most completely and utterly failed.

The club did, in the end, ask me to deliver a lecture devoted exclusively to the problems of translation regarding "The Exile's Letter." Afterward there was a dinner in the club's majestic dining room with a hundred attendees, many of them old-timers from Hong Kong who, like me, would never be going back. The grayheads in our final days of upright slumber. But the atmosphere was jolly. There were many speeches and the food did not matter. I tapped a wineglass, stood before them, and declared, half gone on the house claret, that "The Exile's Letter" was the greatest single poem about friendship ever written outside of Homer and that my lecture would proceed at our tables at my own request—for what could be more fitting to honor the spirit of Li Bai than to eat and drink while listening to it?

I recounted the famous story of his death at the age of sixty, which Jimmy had recalled for me as we were crossing the bridge of St. John's all those years before. Falling into a river during a party while trying to seize a reflected image of the moon, that celestial body forever associated with his work. It may or may not be true. But as I spoke I began to feel a presence that did not correspond with my perceptions. It might have been the claret or the heat in the dining room, or perhaps the presence of Li Bai's ghost. Either way, I was sure that a voyeur had crept in to watch my performance from a distance. It made me fumble my lines and look around the room for clues, though I could only see faithfully inquiring eyes and the waitstaff standing with a monumental gravity by the tables. No one I knew. After my lecture had been concluded I sat down again drenched in sweat and there was awkward applause, as if my audience, too, could feel that I was disturbed. One of the moderators leaned over quietly and asked me if I was all right.

"It's just the heat in here," I said. "I'll settle down."

"Why don't you go outside for a breather?" she suggested.

"All right," I said, gathering myself. "Hold my dessert."

I got up with some difficulty and went outside to the great spiraling marble staircase that plunged down to the club's lobby. The air was full of Victorian dust and the oil portraits on the walls had acquired their nocturnal pallor, which matched the stained-glass heads of Gladstone and colleagues that glowed on the ground floor. The icons of a disappeared civilization. The spiral was so precipitous that it was hard to see anyone rising or descending below, yet as I leaned over the polished banister I caught sight of a man in a houndstooth suit limping severely and beating what appeared to be a hasty retreat. I was sure in that moment that he had slipped out of the dining room and so I followed him down, ready to call out Jimmy's name in that funereal silence. A scarface and a cripple wounded by the same city. But on the floor below he had not waited for me. It was only near the ground-floor lobby itself, filled with a party of members, that he paused for a moment, relented, and turned on his good foot to face me. His face had aged and he had lost the gladsome tilt of his hips. Yet the offhanded amorality was still in the eyes, with the knowledge that at the very last moment I would not have the guts to hunt him down. It was better that way. He instead smiled and flicked a salute with two fingers against his right temple as if to say "Nice lecture, comrade." And then he was gone, slipped away through the crowd and out into the dusk of Whitehall, where the bells were ringing, though of course not for him.

LAWRENCE OSBORNE is the author of seven critically acclaimed novels, including *The Forgiven*, *Hunters in the Dark*, *Beautiful Animals*, and *The Glass Kingdom*, as well as several books of nonfiction, including *The Wet and the Dry* and *Bangkok Days*. The film adaptation of *The Forgiven*, starring Jessica Chastain and Ralph Fiennes, was released in 2021. Osborne has led a nomadic life, living in Paris, New York, Mexico, and Istanbul, and he currently resides in Bangkok.

ABOUT THE TYPE

This book was set in Fournier, a typeface named for Pierre-Simon Fournier (1712–68), the youngest son of a French printing family. He started out engraving woodblocks and large capitals, then moved on to fonts of type. In 1736 he began his own foundry and made several important contributions in the field of type design; he is said to have cut 147 alphabets of his own creation. Fournier is probably best remembered as the designer of St. Augustine Ordinaire, a face that served as the model for the Monotype Corporation's Fournier, which was released in 1925.